Dear Darlene,
I hope you
enjoy this story.
Have a wonderful
Christmas. Maybe
we can see each
other again at another
scrap-away someday.

Luj Niccum

# The Christmas Calendar

*The Christmas Calendar*

# *Dedication*

This book is dedicated to my best friend Susan, who for the past 22 years has been one of the greatest examples to me of true motherhood to help me get my life on the right track. I wrote this story for you, Susan, as a Christmas gift and now it is a gift to everyone else. Thank you for your love and encouragement and most of all your very special friendship.

# Table of Contents

# *December 1st*

It had been years since the warm glow of Christmas filled Catherine Daley's heart. Now the wintry winds of December brought nothing but a chill to her bones and a dread of the dreary days of winter ahead. As she entered her darkened house that cold December 1st evening after an exhausting day at work, she noticed a package at her doorstep.

Puzzled at the sight of an unexpected box, Catherine slowly stooped down and carefully picked it up. "Now who could have sent me this?" Catherine asked as she examined the package in the dim light of night. She fumbled around in the dark trying to turn on the lamp next to the door. Catherine sat down in the recliner and closely inspected the box in the light. As she turned the box, it reflected the light and cast an iridescent glow.

"There is no name on this box yet it is wrapped like a package to be mailed. Could this be a mistake? No one ever sends me things. This is very interesting paper. I've never seen anything like it. It's like brown mailing paper but it has such a shine to it. I don't know what to think. I probably shouldn't open it since I don't know who sent it," Catherine said quietly to herself. She often spoke out loud to herself when at home. It was a habit that helped her deal with the persistent quiet of her lonely residence.

Catherine sighed as she placed the box aside on the table next to the chair. She grabbed the small pile of mail and went through it carefully. The evening's mail consisted of a few bills and a copy of the Readers Digest that she quickly browsed to find an article of interest. She sat there reading in the quiet for a few moments and then nodded off for a short evening nap.

She woke up to the telephone ringing, nervously grabbed the receiver, said hello, and heard nothing but silence for a few seconds at the other end before a voice spoke up. She knew then she was the target of yet another telemarketer trying to make his evening quota. Catherine exasperatedly said no thank you and hung up and shook her head in disgust. She hated talking on the phone and being bothered by complete strangers. After a simple meal of canned soup, crackers, and a tossed salad, Catherine turned on the television set in her living room. She was immediately bombarded by a series of Christmas related commercials and advertisements for upcoming Christmas specials. Shaking her head at the unpleasant reminder of the season, she grabbed the remote.

Flipping through the channels she finally settled on Jeopardy. Her mind focused on asking the proper questions faster than the participants. She smugly beat out the entire team quite a few times. Catherine, who was very well read, would always think at the show's conclusion that she would be a great contestant but that thought always quickly faded away. She spent many a lonely night voraciously devouring novels and biographies. Occasionally she would work on non-fiction books she selected from the library. She preferred reading to television. Tonight was no exception. In the silence, her mind went back to the strange package that showed up on her doorstep. She felt tempted to open the box, but tinges of fear came over her as she touched it.

"I wonder if someone is trying to play a trick on me. What could be in there?" Catherine thought nervously. She cautiously put the package on top of her refrigerator, turned off the lights and went to her bedroom for the night.

The novel Catherine was currently reading was full of interesting twists and political insight so it was hard to put down and she read most of the evening. Finally sleep overtook her. As usual, after a short sleep she woke up. This restlessness occurred many times during the night. She longed for a complete night of sleep. At a quarter to eleven she lay there thinking more of the box with the peculiar wrapping in her kitchen.

"Strange how it wasn't addressed to me. I might consider opening it if at least had my name on it. You never know these days what dangerous things might come in the mail especially when I don't know who the sender is. I probably shouldn't have even brought it in the house!" Catherine exclaimed out loud in the darkness. She tossed and turned in her bed nervously as she started to feel more scared. Anxiety about her lonely shallow existence seemed to always reach a peak during the nocturnal hours of the day. The unknown package provided much fodder for worrisome thoughts but eventually she again drifted off to sleep.

This time her short spell of sleep included a very vivid dream, perhaps the most realistic dream she ever had. In the dream, a small girl with curly blonde hair dressed in a beautiful dress a lovely shade of light yellow that had a very soft appearance and shimmered in the sunshine, approached her doorstep. In her arms she carried a package. It looked just like the package Catherine found on her doorstep that evening. The little girl looked around carefully and cautiously placed the box at the doorstep. She looked up at the house, paused while she brightly smiled, and then turned and skipped away into a soft mist in the distance. Catherine abruptly woke up and gasped.

She recognized at once the face of the child in the dream. It had been years since she laid her eyes on that sweet innocent face. Tears welled up in Catherine's eyes. It was her darling little Jenny.

"What on earth?" Catherine asked herself as she leaned over to pull a tissue from the box on her nightstand table. "That was so real!" she remarked as she wiped her eyes. Now her thoughts turned again to the box and she admitted, "It couldn't be." Catherine felt really frightened as she lay in bed. Her mind became flooded with bittersweet memories. She thought of her children. She pictured her son Jimmy with his freckles and curly red hair and eyes that twinkled with mischief. She never could stay mad at him very long when he caused a ruckus in the home or brought home unwelcome visitors in his pockets. How she longed for his tight hugs and sweet kisses on her cheek. Then her thoughts turned to Susie. What a lovely daughter she was. Kind, generous and helpful and how she loved to play house and be the little mother. What happiness she brought into the home. Then there was little Jenny. How she missed that darling little girl. Jenny had the nickname "Miss Sunshine". She woke up each morning with a big smile on her face. She loved to sing songs and draw pretty pictures for her mommy. Her troubled heart ached as she pondered about the wonderful husband she once had. James was a kind man. His funny sense of humor and jolly laughter made it fun to be in the home when he was there. He did his best to provide for the family and be a help to his busy wife as she did her best to make the home a wonderful place to live. She had tried very hard every day to keep the thoughts of this family out of her mind. Her heart burst with sadness and tears flowed hard and bitterly.

It was a terrible night fifteen years earlier, a few nights before Christmas Eve that her husband drove the children home from a night at the ice skating rink. She remained at home busily wrapping just the right gifts for her children. She had the house beautifully decorated and gifts prepared for her parents, sister, neighbors and other friends. She was sure the reason for the family's delay in getting home on time was a trip to their favorite ice cream parlor. Later that evening she received the dreaded phone call instructing her to go to the hospital. Her daughter Susie lay in a coma but James, Jimmy, and Jenny died in the head on collision. Catherine shuddered as she recalled that horrible scene of her dear daughter wrapped in bandages, hovering near death. The image was so upsetting to Catherine that she immediately got out of her bed and turned on the bedroom lights. She sat on her bed pondering for a minute and then quickly went to the kitchen. She grabbed the package on top of the refrigerator and ripped off the paper in her anguish.

In the darkness of the kitchen she beheld what looked like a box in the shape of a house and it reflected a bit of moonlight coming from the kitchen window. She leaned over and switched on the light. Catherine stood staring at this remarkable gift. It was very beautiful and antique-like. It appeared to be hand-carved out of some kind of rich colored wood, polished smooth, and painted with stunning detail. The shape of the house reminded Catherine of the home she used to live in with her husband and children. This wooden house had many more windows than she remembered her own home having. The windows appeared to be in front of little rooms in the box, like a real home would have. Catherine noticed on each of the windows, there was a number painted in gold. At once she recognized this house was a very unique advent calendar.

Catherine became excited and yet a bit fearful when she realized the window that had the number one painted on it was lit up, like there was someone in the room behind the window. Intrigued yet frightened, Catherine took a deep breath and peered into the little window. What she saw looked just like her own bedroom she had when she was a young girl but in miniature. Catherine recognized the lovely pink bedspread and an assortment of beloved toys on the shelf. Her heart pounded with excitement when she saw the beautiful doll she received for Christmas many years ago sitting at a small table set up with a tiny china tea set.

A flood of warm memories filled Catherine's heart and she recalled the wonderful Christmas when she received the treasured gift and the joy she had when she spent many magical days playing with the doll she named Clara. Catherine eyes welled up with tears as she longed to have such simple joy in her life again. She looked away painfully from the magical little window and glanced around her small dark kitchen and was overcome by the contrast. Her life had become as dark, dreary, and mundane as this little kitchen. Her life was tightly contained as she struggled with her ongoing depression and other mental illnesses.

Catherine recalled the image of little Jenny placing the package on her doorstep in her dream. "Is it really possible Jenny brought this to me? But she is dead. No! It's not possible. This is too much. Am I really going crazy? I must get some sleep," Catherine wondered as she put the calendar on top of the refrigerator, opened the cabinet door containing her sleep-aid medicine and took a double dose with trembling hands. She went and sat down in the living room and flicked on the television set. The late night programming helped draw her mind away from the events of the evening and soon she was asleep in the chair.

# *December 2ⁿᵈ*

Catherine awoke feeling chilled and stiff. Shaking her head in disgust for once again falling asleep in the recliner, she glanced over at the living room clock dimly lit by the pale moonlight. It was still early, well before the time to get up for work. She stumbled out of the chair and made her way back to the bedroom. Catherine's drowsy thoughts turned to the strange little wooden house in her kitchen. She lay in bed and reflected on what feelings were kindled in her heart when she peered into the little window and saw her old bedroom. She really did have a wonderful childhood. How she missed those cherished times of innocence and joy. But then her mind was soon dominated by fearful thoughts. What was going on? How could she have possibly seen her old bedroom like that? What was this advent calendar and how did she get it? Should she get rid of it? Where did it come from?

Who made it? She thought again about the dream which only made her feel more anxious. Cynical thoughts continued to parade though Catherine's churning mind. Catherine began to sweat and breathe harder. Her heart pounded. Catherine's level of anxiety drove her to get up and obtain some medicine out of the cabinet.

Catherine tried desperately not to think of the strange wooden house, the vivid dream of her Jenny, and the sad thoughts of her departed family. She grabbed the book on her bed stand to help return her thoughts to the intriguing novel. Soon it was time to get up and get the day started. Catherine worked at a downtown accounting firm. She was notorious for arriving at the office early and staying late. Working with numbers seemed to completely occupy Catherine's mind. She was obsessed with accuracy. It was one thing in her life that she really could control. She poured over the numbers again and again and had a strong reputation for catching errors of all sorts. Over the years, Catherine became a valuable employee with an excellent performance record. Her life revolved around her work and she found it a refuge of sorts from her pathetic private life and the gnawing feelings of agonizing loneliness.

Catherine was anxious to leave her tiny house that morning. She paced nervously in the cramped kitchen while sipping a cup of tea. She filled a thermos with some leftover soup and a made small ham sandwich in the dim kitchen light, glancing up at the wooden house on top of the refrigerator. Catherine noticed more light coming from it than last night. Her curiosity was aroused.

"Should I look at it again? What if another window is lit up? I can't look at it. I should get rid of it!" Catherine thought. She got her purse and put the lunch in it and then paused as she stared at the little house again.

"What is going on? Why am I so scared? I should look at it again," she determined. With a dash of courage she lifted the wooden house down from the refrigerator and examined it once more. Admiring the exquisite craftsmanship, she discovered another window lit up with the number two printed on it. Catherine pulled it close so she could peer into the newly lit little room. What she saw this time was a tiny baby cradle. She vaguely recognized the furniture. She studied the small room carefully for any other signs of familiarity. The room was bare except for the cradle. Catherine then noticed a baby blanket in the cradle and knew at once it belonged to her baby sister.

Suddenly all her thoughts were turned to her little sister. How she had begged her parents for a sister! She prayed to God for a sister. She had been the only child for five years. Then right before Christmas, her little sister was born. She loved baby Christina so much. Catherine was a wonderful big sister. She spent many enjoyable hours playing with Christina who she nicknamed Tina. Even though Catherine was quite a bit older, the girls grew to be very close as sisters all through their childhood. As Catherine pondered those wonderful years spent with Tina, she thought about her sister now. She hadn't talked to Tina in years.

Catherine recalled the last conversation she had with Tina. It had been several years since the accident and Catherine's life was in shambles. Her daughter remained in a coma and family pressure was on to shut off life support. Doctors gave little hope of Susie ever regaining consciousness as she had very little brain activity. Tina at first tried to be supportive of Catherine decision to go along with the doctor's advice but she later disagreed. This put a great strain on the sister's relationship. A horrible argument ensued with deeply embedded guilt from Catherine fueling ugly accusations against her sister and a strong resolution to cease speaking to her anymore. The intense emotional pain of the entire situation triggered a nervous breakdown in Catherine. She cut off all communication to her sister and any family members. She refused to return calls and sent back all mail. She relocated to a new state to live in reclusion. Her wish for a life of seclusion was granted.

Catherine's heart stung with intense pain. She closed her eyes and quietly wept. She put the house back and grabbed her things and quickly left the house. The house was successfully dredging up deeply buried feelings and memories. Catherine felt stabbed in the heart. She sobbed all the way to work. She sat in her car in the parking lot waiting for some emotional strength. It took a while but she regained her composure and focus. Work was all Catherine allowed herself to think about and soon she was in her office beginning her long workday.

Co-workers noticed Catherine's red eyes and began to quietly gossip among themselves about the possible reasons for the evidence of hard crying. Catherine had a very strong reputation for being stoic. She had no close friends at work. All the accounting firm knew about Catherine was the intensely professional manner she displayed and her dedication to perfection. She was a closed book otherwise.

Catherine tried her best to keep thoughts of the advent calendar out of her number filled head. She succeeded until lunchtime when she noticed that someone had put a cute paper Christmas advent calendar in the work lunchroom. She purposely sat down at a table distance away so she wouldn't have to see it. A curious co-worker walked by and saw Catherine sitting by herself.

"Hi Catherine, how are you doing?" Alice asked as she sat down next to Catherine. Alice was a friendly middle-aged office assistant who always said hello to Catherine.

"I'm fine," Catherine answered quickly.

"Can I join you for lunch?" Alice asked. Catherine looked surprised and a bit uncomfortable. She rarely had any company in the lunchroom. She nodded. Alice left for a few minutes and then returned with a microwavable frozen entrée that she put in the microwave. Soon she joined Catherine at the table. "I hope this is better than the one I had yesterday!" Alice joked. Catherine smiled.

"I was kind of wondering, Catherine, if everything is okay? I mean, I can tell you've been crying pretty hard. You're not one to show any emotion, so you have all of us here worried about you!" Alice mentioned as she patted Catherine's hand. Alice got up to retrieve her lunch in the microwave. Catherine collected her thoughts and sighed. "Is everything okay at home?" Alice asked. Catherine paused before she spoke.

"Yes. Everything is fine," responded Catherine who forced a smile and nodded.

"Well, that's a relief. Things have been so crazy here at work lately haven't they? And now it's Christmas again. I don't know how I am going to find any extra time to shop and do all the things this hectic holiday season demands!" declared Alice shaking her head, "are you ready for Christmas?"

"Oh, I don't do much for Christmas anymore, I keep it very simple," Catherine replied while looking down at her thermos of soup.

"That's always my intention but I never seem to achieve it! What's your secret?"

Catherine looked sternly at Alice before replying.

"It helps to not have a family," Catherine answered quietly. Alice nodded.

"Families are very demanding, that's true. Half of my family is grown up but it's my rowdy teenagers who still hang around the house that really does me in. I need to say no more to their demands and get more of their help. Some days I really dread going home!" Alice said with a chuckle.

"I understand that," confessed Catherine realizing she had a completely different reason for dreading her home. To keep the subject of the conversation off her, Catherine quickly asked, "Well, how many children do you have?"

"Six total. Can you believe that? What was I thinking? We have two girls in college right now. Our oldest son graduated in engineering last year and now has a job at his father's business. I have two teenage sons, ages 16 and 14 and my youngest daughter is 12 almost 13. Phew. It makes me tired just to think about it," Alice acknowledged and then she laughed. Catherine looked up at the clock and decided lunch was over.

"Thanks for spending your lunch with me. Have a nice day," Catherine said to Alice as she abruptly got up from the table.

"See you later," replied Alice after she swallowed a bite of her lunch. Catherine glanced at the wall and regretted seeing the paper advent calendar again. A long time ago, Catherine made it a tradition to hang an advent calendar at the beginning of December. She enjoyed opening a door each day for the twenty-four days preceding Christmas day. She even made her children an adorable countdown to Christmas advent calendar, which they dearly loved. Now advent calendars were just another painful reminder of the dreaded days before Christmas. Her mind flashed back to the two lit miniature windows and once again tears welled up in her eyes. She quickly escaped notice by heading immediately for the ladies room. Grabbing a bit of toilet paper to dab her moist eyes, she leaned against the wall of the stall and sighed heavily. It would be a long difficult afternoon if she couldn't get these thoughts out of her mind. She focused on the tasks waiting completion in her office and soon she was once again hard at work at her desk.

# *December 3rd*

Catherine found it difficult to go home the previous evening so she opted to have dinner at her favorite restaurant and stayed late reading her novel. When she came inside her dark little house, she didn't even go into the kitchen but headed straight for her bedroom. It was close to 11:30 P.M. when she finally fell asleep. Now she found herself staring at the glowing alarm clock in the darkness of her bedroom. It read 3:30 A.M. How Catherine longed for a complete night of sleep, now more than ever. A long sigh was followed by a series of persistent worried thoughts that occupied her mind like a string of annoying television commercials right before a favorite program.

"Enough!" Catherine heard herself say in the darkness. "I am crazier than ever, I am sure of it. I must call my shrink tomorrow and make sure he has my doses correct!" She took another dose of medicine for her growing anxiety and grabbed the novel that was close to completion.

The early morning hours passed quickly as she finished up the novel. Catherine dozed off towards the end of the book. The little amount of sleep she got only covered the last remaining hour of the night. Soon Catherine was up and readying herself for another workday, like a cog in a wheel. Catherine had dug herself quite a deep rut with her entire life revolving around work. She had no real friends to speak of anymore. She avoided her neighbors. She was always unresponsive when the grocery clerk or others in the community tried to make conversation. After a while, most people gave up on any effort to speak to her and she was satisfied with the island of silence she had created for herself. When any feelings of loneliness crept into her brain, she always turned her thoughts towards an issue at work or the latest novel she was reading. It provided a safe harbor for her mind and a way to detach from the painful feelings of her heart. Catherine existed from day to day and it seemed that wintertime had settled permanently in her confined miserable world.

Catherine glanced nervously at the peculiar little wooden house perched on top of her refrigerator as she fixed her eggs. Once again, it appeared that more light was emanating from the unusual advent calendar. For a time, Catherine resisted the urge to take it down and examine it. As she read the morning newspaper, she kept glancing up at it. She felt her curiosity growing.

"I am never going to get my mind off that bizarre thing until I look at it once more."

At first glance, the newly lit window didn't appear to have anything inside. She looked again at the first two windows and once again she felt her heart burn with a mixture of joy and sorrow. Her eyes began to mist over. Catherine's thoughts immediately focused on her sister Tina. She wondered where she might be living now and if she ever got married to her boyfriend. Catherine could feel her heart soften a tiny amount. Upon her return to the third window, she noticed some objects on a tiny little couch that looked like the one she remembered having in the living room where she grew up. The knitting needles, ball of yarn, and a light pink sweater all looked very familiar to Catherine. Now she remembered getting a beautiful pink sweater for Christmas one year that she adored. Her mother must have lovingly made that sweater for her because the sweater had the same color as the yarn sitting on the couch.

"Oh, how I loved that sweater! I didn't know Mom made that for me," Catherine admitted out loud as she reminisced about that particular Christmas when she was eight years old. Her parents were poor but they did all they could to make Christmas a magical and happy celebration. Catherine thought sadly about her mother. Although the teenage years had put a strain on the mother daughter relationship, overall she had happy memories of her mother as a child. Before the accident, Catherine and her family went to visit Catherine's parents several times a year. She had a good relationship with them. The accident changed all that. The strain of the long hospitalization of her daughter and the devastating medical decision that had to be made led to Catherine's nervous breakdown. She felt deeply disappointed by her parents during this time. They had their own health and financial crises that prevented them from being a major support to Catherine. She resented terribly their apparent indifference to her situation. Through this emotional hurricane of hurt and resentment, Catherine had decided to cut off her relationship with her parents and her sister. Things really didn't get better as the years went by. Correspondence from Catherine to her parents deteriorated to the level of an annual Christmas card with a brief business like message sometimes with no return address. Her parents were deeply hurt and resentful of their daughter's indifference. They were confused by Catherine's need for complete isolation. The chasm created by the lack of forgiveness and communication grew deeper each year.

As she stared at the pretty pink yarn on the little couch, she wondered how her mother was really doing and started to feel a longing to talk to her and hear her voice once again.

"How many years has it been? Maybe I should call her?' Catherine wondered. "She probably wouldn't want to hear from me. I am the basket-case daughter!" Catherine shuddered as she recalled the last conversation she had with her mother years ago on the phone remembering her mother calling her a basket case. This was in response to a horrid and painful accusation from Catherine. What it was all about Catherine couldn't even recall now. Only the pain remained in her memory. Slowly she put the house back on top of the refrigerator and wiped her eyes. Her thoughts returned to the calendar itself. How was all of this possible? It was mystifying to Catherine. She got out her phone book and called her doctor's office to set up another appointment. She left a message to have the office call her at work later.

Work was a welcome relief to her troubled mind that morning. Occasionally she pondered the thought of calling her folks but quickly dismissed the possibility. What would she say to them? Catherine was grateful to find out her doctor had an opening late that afternoon and looked forward to seeing him again. Over the years, she had become quite close to her psychiatrist, Dr. Wayne Thomas. He had seen her though the very roughest times of her mental breakdown and depression. At the doctor's office later that day, Catherine decided to spill the beans about the calendar. All Dr. Thomas did was nod quietly and take a few notes.

"Well? Dr. Thomas, say something!" Catherine exclaimed, "Am I mad? Is this really possible? I mean a calendar that shows me stuff from my past?"

"Let's see what level I have your anti-psychotics meds at," Dr. Thomas responded. Catherine felt distraught and uncomfortable with her doctor for the first time. She felt disappointed that he didn't comment on the reality of the calendar but seemed to dismiss it as a psychotic episode. Then Catherine felt a great sense of unease. Maybe she had been imagining the whole thing! It was one of those terribly awkward moments that cause one to reflect on reality. As she sat gazing out the window of the doctor's office she seriously wondered if she was dreaming all of this. Had any of it been real?

"But it seems so real!" Catherine thought to herself as tears began to well up in her eyes.

"It's possible that you could imagine such things, Catherine, but I seriously doubt any *reality* to it," Dr. Thomas concluded finally, "it's just not possible. I do have your Thorazine levels a bit lowered so I will go ahead and up your prescription a bit and that should help you deal with this episode you are having. Catherine, it's the holidays and a very typical time to have psychotic episodes about memories. I recall having a conversation with you about something similar a few years ago. Let me go check my records. I'll be right back," Dr. Thomas got up and left the office for a moment. Catherine nervously drummed her fingers in his absence, trying her best to believe the good doctor.

"Yes, here it is. It was in December several years ago. You were having mild psychotic episodes at night. You thought you saw large spiders in your bedroom at night. At other times you claimed to have people in your room. Does that sound familiar?" Dr. Thomas asked as he looked up from the chart. Catherine's cheeks flamed bright red with the recollection. For a moment, there was awkward silence as Catherine reflected on the past several days' events. First finding the unusual package, the dream of Jenny so vivid and real, then the subsequent windows of the calendar house lit with scenes from her past in miniature. How it triggered so much emotion in her heart! She recalled the nights of waking up by the sudden trauma of seeing rather large spiders descending from the ceiling towards her. They too seemed so real. Seeing people in her room at night also seemed real, like they were there to speak to her but she never heard a thing. It was quite frightening for Catherine. Once the doctor prescribed the additional medication, the nightmarish episodes disappeared. Catherine compared the two experiences and then shook her head.

"No, Dr. Thomas, they are totally different. Yes, I did imagine the spiders and people to the point they seemed completely real. I believe now they weren't actually there even though at the time it seemed that way to me. It was in my head, totally. But this is different. I held the package. I have it in my kitchen. You can come see if you'd like, or better yet I will bring it in for you to see," Catherine responded.

"That will be fine. Catherine, are you under a lot of stress from work? Are you getting enough sleep at night?" Dr. Thomas inquired.

"Work is busy but not particularly stressful. I do not sleep well and the prescription you gave me doesn't seem powerful enough. I've had to increase my dose several times to get any effect," Catherine answered. Dr. Thomas scribbled an additional prescription for her and soon she was driving home. Catherine's mind was flooded with thoughts about her doctor's response. Maybe this was just another psychotic episode that would disappear as soon as she took the additional medicine he had prescribed for her. When she returned home, she heated up a frozen dinner in the microwave. Catherine avoided the calendar in the kitchen and turned on the evening news.

# *December 4ᵗʰ*

Catherine slept more soundly than usual with an increased level of sleeping medication. When she returned home the previous evening from the doctor's office, she tried her best to stop thinking about the calendar and her family before bed. She was very nervous that the entire experience was merely another psychotic episode in her life. Taking the calendar to her doctor's office would help remove any doubt. Catherine felt sure about this. Once she convinced her doctor that she was not imagining it, he could help her figure out what was going on. That helped Catherine relax as she succumbed to the effects of the latest prescriptions.

As usual, she woke up early but felt more refreshed than previous mornings. She stared at the patterns on her bedroom wall made from the outside streetlights and the branches of the trees that swayed in the nighttime wind. Her mind traveled back in time for a moment to her childhood when she would often wake up at night. The noise of branches scraping at the side of the house during storms would really frighten her. Most of the time she would cry out and eventually, one of her parents would come to console her. She recalled one time when her dad turned on her bedside lamp and read her a short bedtime story. Catherine smiled in the darkness at the comforting memory. Lying in bed, Catherine began to feel that quiet longing once more to connect with her parents. Feelings of guilt, anger, frustration, and worry quickly drove it out of her heart.

Before long she was into her usual morning routine. Catherine studied herself in the dimly lit bathroom mirror. Middle age was becoming more apparent on her face day by day. Her dark blonde hair had begun to show streaks of gray and she considered a hair coloring appointment to hide it.

"Oh, what's the use? Who cares?" Catherine mumbled to herself. Thick bifocal glasses helped hide the more obvious wrinkles around her eyes. Frown lines dug deep into her forehead from hours of determination and focus pouring over and correcting numbers. She had a narrow face with deep-set bluish green eyes. She wore no makeup. She rationalized that nobody really paid her any attention anyways so it was just a waste of time and money. Her hair was shoulder length with enough body to look manageable without a lot of attention except for an occasional haircut. Her wardrobe was simple but very business-like. She seemed to finally have her weight under control somewhat. For years she was terribly underweight as part of her severe depression. After losing her family, she lost all interest in eating. Now she made eating simply a part of her daily routine, like showing up for work early and staying late.

Once upon a time, Catherine's closet was filled with more fashionable and fun outfits. She never went out of the home without her face done up. It seemed like her husband always noticed when she spent time on her appearance. He would tell her she was very beautiful so it always seemed worthwhile. Now she stared at the plain aging face in the mirror with complete indifference.

As she entered the kitchen, she took her morning dose of Thorazine along with her other medications. Half wanting the calendar to instantly vanish from her sight as if it really was in her imagination, she turned to look up at it. It was still there and glowing brighter than the day before. Catherine let out a big sigh.

"I've got to take that thing to Dr. Thomas," She said with resolve as she reached up to grab it to inspect the fourth window. In the window she saw a half built green bicycle. She recognized it at once as one of her favorite things from her childhood. How she had begged and begged for a bike! Knowing how her parents scrimped and saved, Catherine was once again reminded of the kind sacrifices her parents made for her growing up. She pictured her father putting together the bike. He loved to tinker in the garage and build things.

"He lovingly built this bike for me," Catherine thought. She never realized his hands made this most special gift. Her father worked long and hard hours at his factory job and was rarely home. Tears once more welled up in her eyes and felt her heart ache within her. Catherine thought sadly about her parents. She glanced back at the window with the pink sweater in it once more, and sobbed quietly. She grabbed a paper sack and stuffed the wooden house inside. She put it by the front door so she wouldn't forget to put it in her car.

The weather outside was as cold as Catherine could remember. Dark gray clouds hung heavily in the early morning sky. Catherine shivered as an icy chill penetrated her coat and freezing wind whipped about her as she got in her car. It seemed that amidst the brutal winter weather descending on that cold December day, there in Catherine's heart, long formed icicles were slowly beginning to melt.

Thoughts of her parents from her childhood flowed freely into her mind and she didn't force them away. For the first time in years, she seriously determined to call them. A battle was mounting in her mind with the usual negative thoughts opposing such an action. She had so successfully kept her family out of her life for so long; the thought of really facing them once again was terrifying. There was an enormous whirlpool of guilt, resentment, and anguish swirling about within her that Catherine didn't think she could ever face them again. Yet, there remained in her mind, a thread of hope and desire that continued to linger and slowly grow.

At lunch, Catherine drove her car carefully on the streets covered with a few inches of snow over to Dr. Thomas's office. She had called ahead to make sure he was there during her lunch break and reminded him of the calendar house she wanted to show him. Now she wished she had stayed at the office as the snow was falling hard on the windshield making the driving treacherous. She glanced over at the wooden house inside the paper bag perched on the passenger seat beside her. It continued to glow. Once again, she admired the incredible craftsmanship of the house. She had never seen anything made out of wood quite so exquisite. Catherine thought that the beauty of the workmanship would impress Dr. Thomas.

She made her way carefully into the parking lot and trudged through the deepening snow to his office. Once inside the building, she shook off the snow from her coat and headed up the elevator. She asked the receptionist to let Dr. Thomas know she had arrived. Catherine nervously drummed her fingers on the couch armrest waiting for Dr. Thomas to emerge.

"He seems to be in no hurry to see me," she thought. Just as she stood up to grab a nearby magazine, he came out into the waiting room.

"Hello Catherine. How are you doing today? I see that you brought me the calendar house. Please come into my office."

Catherine smiled and grabbed the bag, following the large doctor into the office. Once inside, she reached into the bag and presented the wooden house to the doctor and announced, "Isn't this beautiful?" He took it into his hands and stared at it for a minute. He turned it over and handed it back to Catherine. He said nothing but got out some medical forms and started writing on them. Catherine stared at him in disbelief. Finally she spoke, "Dr. Thomas, what do you think of it?" He ignored her for a minute as he finished writing. Catherine could feel the anger grow inside of her. "Why is he putting me off?" she thought.

Finally Dr. Thomas explained, "Catherine, I have some paperwork here that I need you to sign. I am admitting you to the West Valley Mental Care Facility. I think it is in your best interest at this time."

She stared at the paperwork and felt her heart drop.

"Dr. Thomas, what do you mean?" Catherine anxiously asked, "Why do you want to admit me to a mental hospital? What did you think of the wooden calendar house?"

"Catherine, I am afraid you have slipped into an unusual case of mental delusion. The wooden calendar house is just a piece of wood, nothing else! I am concerned that the current medications you are taking are not able to help your brain decipher reality, and perhaps may even be triggering this episode. You need additional treatment I'm afraid. This facility is best equipped to help a person like you," Dr. Thomas answered coldly.

Catherine stared at the floor in complete shock. Tears burned in her eyes. Once again, she began to mentally question her own sense of reality. Was she truly losing her mind? Had all of this incredible loneliness and emotional anguish finally sent her over the brink? She sat down on the couch, tightly folded her arms, and began to sob. Dr. Thomas went over to his desk, looked up the number of the hospital, and began calling to set up arrangements for Catherine's hospital stay.

Catherine shook her head while she cried. She had terrible memories of mental hospitals. She had spent several weeks in one when she first had her mental breakdown. That was an experience she never wanted to relive again! She also spent a week in a facility when her depression brought her down to a suicide attempt. That is when she met Dr. Thomas. He had helped her and she became quite attached to him. Now she just stared at him in disbelief.

Catherine looked down at the calendar house sitting on the couch beside her. It looked as real to her as anything did in that room. The four little windows shined with light. Each had gold numeral lettering on the window written in a beautiful old-fashioned script. The wood was hand carved, smoothed and polished. It glowed with an unusual luster. The eaves and window shutters looked so familiar to her. Surely it was replica of the house owned by her and her husband James once upon a time. She looked lovingly upon the beautiful little house with the mysterious windows. She touched it and felt a warm feeling calm her troubled heart. At that moment, a thought came into her mind. This was her gift. Her private gift and it was not to be shared with anyone. A sense of incredible wonder came over her.

"Perhaps, only my eyes see what it truly is, to everyone else, it's just a piece of wood!" Catherine thought hopefully and she mentioned this realization to Dr. Thomas. This convinced him further that Catherine was in need of serious treatment, and he pressed her to check in for at least one night for further examination. She reluctantly agreed to go but held on to that comforting thought.

# *December 5th*

Catherine awoke in the strange room and looked about her. The room was simple and consisted of a single bed, a nightstand, and an overhead light. One painting of a vase of roses adorned the wall and heavy curtains covered the reinforced opaque window. The room reminded her of a previous stay at a mental hospital. About 10 years earlier, the stress of everything had finally taken its toll on her will to keep going. Catherine had simply given into hopelessness and took all of her medicine at once. Luckily, her neighbor Carol had managed to find her in time and rushed her to the hospital. She spent a week in recovery and then another week at the mental hospital. It was a hard long climb out of the deep abyss of despair but Catherine improved day by day and with the help of her doctor, was able to get a tighter grip on her life. She determined to be successful at her new occupation and put the incident behind her. Taking things one day at a time and trying to forget about her tragic past enabled Catherine to go on. She thought less and less about her departed family both living and dead, and poured her heart and soul into her new job.

How things had turned again with the mysterious gift showing up at her doorstep. Catherine struggled to not think about the images she had seen in the little windows. The experiences with the one-of-a-kind advent calendar were haunting her mind. The memories of her past had been well tucked away and the calendar was stirring up those painful emotional embers. She wanted those painful scorching embers put out. Guilty feelings soon began to overcome her and she once again contemplated contacting her parents. The desire was quickly negated. She lay quietly agonizing in her bed.

Recollections of the previous day soon filled her mind. The psychiatric counseling she endured occupied her thoughts. She began to be convinced that the advent calendar house was only a piece of wood, nothing more. Yesterday she had the thought that the wooden house was somehow for her viewing only. Today she felt different. Her faint belief had dissolved into doubt. She squelched any feelings of tenderness in her heart and dismissed any illogical thoughts. Catherine just wanted to return back to her normal life and forget the past four days ever happened. She would endure the barrage of psychiatric examinations that accompanied a stay in a mental health facility with no further mention of a wooden house. She would be released in no time. She held fast to the conviction that she wasn't losing her hard fought level of sanity after all. She would simply put it out of her mind and get back to working hard. She convinced herself that she never wanted to see that wooden house again and she didn't care who had it now.

The day wore on. She complied well with the doctors' counsel to put the whole thing out of her mind. She sat reading in bed trying to focus on the story and fighting any thoughts concerning her life at the moment. She seemed to be pacifying Dr. Thomas' concerns and felt confident he would soon release her. He nevertheless adjusted her medications to help prevent any further episodes. He also added a new medication. In the afternoon dose of medication, a tranquilizer was included and Catherine obliged. Sleep soon overcame her.

Her sleep was anything but tranquil. She found herself lost in a mist. Feelings of great despair overcame Catherine. For what seemed like hours, she wandered aimlessly. Finally she stumbled upon a building. Catherine felt around for a door but only encountered glass windows. Desperately trying to get inside the structure to escape the mist, she felt a person brush past her. She turned to see who it was and saw no one. Now she could only hear footsteps inside, and then children's laughter. She banged on the

Catherine but found it extremely difficult to maintain a close friendship with her as Catherine descended into the dark abyss of her mental breakdown. Catherine tried to recall the last time she had spoken to Peggy. It was all too vague to her now. She had not received a phone call or a letter from her in years. Did Peggy even care about her anymore?

This was just another painful reminder of her pathetic life. Catherine struggled in every way. She longed to be free of all this pain. She had tried with all her might to bury it deep and thought she was successful but those agonizing feelings were still so very present. Had Catherine not adored and centered her life on her family so much, it might have been easier to take when they left her. Catherine had intensely loved her family. There was a massive hole in Catherine's life. It was created when her family died suddenly that horrible day so many years ago, followed by the lingering tragedy of Susie's coma and death. All that remained was a scarred and devastated heart, one that was almost past feeling.

Dr. Thomas suddenly entered the room and caught Catherine off guard. She tried to hide the wooden house but she wasn't quick enough and Dr. Thomas immediately noticed it.

"Why Catherine, what is that doing in here?" Dr. Thomas asked.

"I don't know," Catherine answered quietly, trying her best to not show any emotion. He came over and grabbed it from her. She didn't resist.

"I thought we agreed that it's best if you don't have this piece of wood anymore," Dr. Thomas noted sternly, "I'd like to keep you here for at least one more day, possibly two now that I see you can't seem to let go of that wood. Catherine, it is essential for you to let go of such delusions."

"I know Dr. Thomas. I am trying. I don't know how that got back into my room, honest. I was sleeping and I had a strange dream about the house I have been telling you about and I woke up suddenly and I saw it there by the door. Maybe some hospital staff put it there?" Catherine suggested.

"I don't think so but I will inquire. Can you tell me about the dream? Do you remember it?"

"It was very real. What I remember is being lost in a dark mist for what seemed like an interminably long time and I felt very frightened. The other part I remember is walking next to a building, which I couldn't see because of the mist. I felt around trying to find a door but I only felt glass. At that time, the mist vanished and I looked and recognized the building as my home that I lived in with my husband and children many years ago. It was very big and I felt very small. That was so strange," Catherine explained. She began to speak of seeing the lit up windows but stopped before she said anything about seeing Jimmy. She ceased from sharing anything further.

"Is there more?" Dr. Thomas asked. Catherine shook her head. She then regretted her response as Dr. Thomas seemed even more convinced that Catherine needed more therapy. He wrote on her chart for a few minutes and then looked up at her.

"I don't think you're ready to leave here," Dr. Thomas answered flatly.

"But Dr. Thomas, I feel completely different about the house, I mean, wood. I don't think it is a house. I think it's just …," Catherine answered quietly but Dr. Thomas interrupted her, not convinced.

"You need to stay here."

Catherine sat in her bed pondering the dream after the doctor left the room. Feeling now like a prisoner, she wanted to go home. She wished she could see the paper dolls in the window once again because they had triggered a happy feeling in her heart. Her thoughts turned to her friend Peggy. She felt an urge to call her old friend. Tears welled up in her eyes as she grabbed the phone but then realized she had absolutely no idea where Peggy might be living now. Catherine sadly put down the receiver, looked around at the dreary hospital room, and quietly sobbed.

# *December 6ᵗʰ*

Catherine lay in bed struggling to wake up and feeling very depressed. Catherine had been dealing with severe depression on and off for many years since the accident. She hadn't felt this bad in a very long time. She felt much darkness inside and despair pressing down on her. Even her hospital room seemed darker than before. She had taken some sleep medication last night as prescribed by Dr. Thomas. He wanted to make sure she had a deep sleep uncomplicated by any further dreams that only seemed to prolong this delusional episode. Dr. Thomas had concluded that Catherine had imagined this whole thing to bring her comfort as the Christmas season approached. He was very aware of the deep loneliness she felt and he often mentioned things she could to do to alleviate those feelings. Catherine would agree with his ideas but never follow through on any of his suggestions.

She had no dreams the previous night that she could recall and felt very groggy from the sleep medication. She got up and tried to look through the opaque glass window to the world outside. She longed to be outside and back at work again. This unexpected leave from work put extra stress on her situation as she thought of several assignments that still needed to be completed. It seemed to be snowing again. More snow falling only made Catherine feel more depressed. She hated snow along with everything else that December brought. She leaned her head against the cold windowpane. The feeling of the glass immediately reminded her of the dream she had yesterday.

"Is it really possible that I concocted this whole thing up in my mind? But that doesn't explain how the mysteriously wrapped package showed up on my door. That wood had to come from somewhere," Catherine wondered to herself and sighed.

"Maybe someone is playing a trick on me, but who? I've got to figure a way of getting out of here, today if possible. At least I didn't have any more strange dreams last night. What will convince Dr. Thomas that I am better when I feel like my whole world is caving in and I don't feel like it's even worth saving?" Catherine pondered despondently.

Catherine's attention was drawn to the pattern the falling snowflakes were making on the window outside. They seemed so light and carefree as they gently landed. Once upon a time,

Catherine used to yearn for snow in December. She delighted at the appearance of white ice crystals glistening and fluttering in the sky. For a moment, she left her dark room and her mind wandered back to a magical Christmas that was white with lots of snow. That day the family had a joyous time sledding, rolling and decorating jolly snowmen, and building snow forts with other children in the neighborhood. Later, they all bundled up and went on a sleigh ride through the mountains. Catherine remembered the ringing of the jingle bells mixed with children's laughter. Catherine paused on this memory, which hadn't been recalled for many years. The joyful memory lingered in her lonely mind longer than normal but soon a wave of depression seemed to sweep it out.

Before long, Catherine would meet once again with trained professionals assigned to help her. What could she say to convince them to let her be released? Dr. Thomas seemed almost adamant that Catherine should remain at the hospital. She didn't know what to think about Dr. Thomas anymore. She had such a trust built up with him for many years but now he seemed so cold and distant about everything. Maybe another doctor would be more reasonable. Catherine decided she would change doctors as soon as possible. But even that thought caused her much uneasiness because Dr. Thomas had been such a central part of her life and a security too. She slipped back into indecision about the situation and decided to think about something else. Sadly, her mind ventured back to the images of the tiny rooms. Once again, Catherine pondered on what it all could mean. Why was she suddenly having such realistic dreams? This had never occurred before in her life. Catherine was sure of that fact. It was quite disturbing to her.

Catherine was in the habit of pushing difficult thoughts out of her mind that might trigger any emotional response. She was quite good at it. The events of the past five days were enough to occupy her mind constantly if she would let them remain. The subject of death had always troubled her, and now it seemed to preoccupy her thoughts. The uncertainty of it and life in general created uncomfortable thoughts and feelings for Catherine. Her mind was dark with prolonged grief. The heaviness of the depression just made things worse. The tragedy of losing one's entire family to it made death seem like a black hole that all would inevitably succumb to. Once upon a time she believed in God and heaven but the bitterness of her long and painful ordeal shattered any faith she had. Catherine, in anger, turned her heart away from God, despite urgings to turn to Him from family and friends. Still, there was a tiny sliver of hope that remained embedded in her heart that she couldn't get rid of, no matter how dark and gloomy things were in her life. If there were a heaven, surely her precious family would be there.

Seeing little Jenny in the mist during that first vivid dream, as beautiful and sweet as ever, like she never died, made Catherine hope that she just went to live somewhere else and didn't really disappear forever. She looked happier than Catherine had ever remembered seeing her. Little Jenny always made Catherine's heart feel light and warm. How Catherine longed to feel that light and warmth again. Then she thought of the look on Jimmy's face, as he looked at her from a darkened window in her last dream. It wasn't one of joy or happiness but one of deep concern and sadness. Catherine pondered on the possible meaning of such sadness coming from such a carefree and energetic person as Jimmy once was. He used to drive her crazy with his messiness and search and destroy ways in the home. He was always in to something new and exploring the world around him with amazing enthusiasm. Catherine could always imagine him someday becoming an explorer or some great inventor. The sad irony of his life being cut so short was that he never became anything. Catherine sighed deeply and refused to think any longer on her departed loved ones.

Catherine thought darkly about her life. It was miserable. It was like living in a shallow suffocating hole. She had dug this hole. There was no real reason to go on like this. She stumbled back to her bed and called the nurse to see if she could get more sleep medication to escape the agonizing and overpowering feelings of despair. Catherine realized, as she lay there in bed, she was in living in her own hell. She wanted out.

Soon Dr. Thomas appeared in her room.

"Why do you want more sleep medication, Catherine?" Dr. Thomas inquired.

"I can't stand how I feel, Dr. Thomas. I want to escape. Last night I had neither dreams nor thoughts. I liked the absence of pain," Catherine answered bluntly.

"Is it because we removed the object of your obsession and delusion?" Dr. Thomas further asked.

Catherine looked at him thoughtfully and said, "No. That's not the reason. It is all of the pain that object has managed to summon in me. I can't stand it! I just want to go back to the way I was before that thing showed up at my door, that's all. I was able to manage my life. I just can't deal with this mountain of pain pulling me down. I feel very sorrowful and dark. I just can't keep going on like this!"

Catherine began to sob. It had been a long time since this stoic woman demonstrated such obvious emotion to anyone and Dr. Thomas made note of it. With everything else troubling her, Catherine also appeared to be suicidal again. He left her room to check her medical records for currently prescribed anti-depression medications.

"I think I would like you to try a stronger anti-depressant medication that was just approved by the F.D.A. I have read some great things about it and it might be just what you need to snap out of this decline," Dr. Thomas said as he reappeared in the doorway after a few minutes. "I'm very concerned to hear you speak about your life in this way again. It's been quite a while since I've heard such language from you."

"I know," Catherine answered sadly, "I'm trying to put all of this behind me but those images are just so strong in my mind and to see all of those reminders of what a wonderful life I once had. Look at my life now. It's just not worth it anymore!"

Silence filled the room for several minutes as Dr. Thomas scribbled on his clipboard occasionally glancing at his distraught patient as she sobbed quietly and clutched the institutional blanket in her hands.

"I'd like to try this medication on you immediately. I am very concerned and I am putting you on a suicide watch until you improve," Dr. Thomas said as he left the room once again.

Catherine shook her head in disbelief. She seemed to be getting worse by the minute instead of getting better. She had to get a handle on things. She was confused about the house and how she felt about it. On the one hand, she longed to hold it and experience once more the comfort she felt when she first thought it might be for her viewing only. On the other hand, that feeling of comfort was becoming so vague while painful thoughts encompassed her mind that Catherine got angry at the house for what it was doing to her sanity. Still, Catherine wondered what image would appear in the sixth window if she did have the calendar house in her hands once again. Back and forth Catherine struggled with what to think about the house. She wondered where it might be at this moment. Did it get thrown away? Why should she care? Why couldn't she just stop thinking about it altogether?

Catherine lay back down in bed and closed her eyes and tried carefully to push it all out of her thoughts when an image of the calendar house appeared in her mind with amazing clarity. It was as if a television screen appeared before her eyes. In her shock at seeing the calendar house once again without having it in her possession, she was both frightened and intrigued. As clearly as if she held it in her hands, Catherine could see into the sixth window, which was now lit. She saw a scene of a living room, all decorated for Christmas. At first, Catherine failed to recognize the room but after a moment, she remembered spending a Christmas there many years ago when she was away at college. The house belonged to the parents of her roommate, Cindy. That year, Catherine's parents were unable to afford for her to come home for the holidays so Cindy's parents graciously offered to have Catherine come spend it with them. She had a marvelous time in this home and felt happy to be there despite missing her own home and parents very much. Catherine felt a longing to be there with Cindy again, wishing she hadn't lost touch with this dear friend as well. As quickly as this image had appeared in her mind, once she recognized the scene, it vanished.

# *December 7th*

Catherine was heavily sedated after she reacted violently to the image, which had suddenly appeared and disappeared in her mind the previous day. The image was so abrupt and vivid it caused Catherine to greatly fear that she was truly losing her mind. She started to scream and cry. She went berserk in her room and tried to escape. Her eyes were filled with terror. The hospital staff was forced to use strong sedatives to calm her down.

Catherine had slept heavily during the night and was monitored closely by staff for any signs of more aberrant behavior. Catherine awoke and looked around the room. Her memory was flooded with the scenes from the previous day. She lay still. Tears moistened her eyes. Her thoughts returned to the reality of the image in her mind and what it could possibly mean. She didn't feel so tense about it today as a result of the heavy sedation she was under.

Was her mind making this entire thing up? Catherine wondered. How could that image appear in her mind like that? She had to have imagined the whole thing. It was the only logical explanation. She would convince Dr. Thomas that she believed everything really was in her head from the very beginning. From now on she would manage things better. No more imaginary calendar houses showing up at her door. They simply didn't exist anywhere but in her mind. The dreams were proof of that and the image of the sixth room proved that too. The dreams were concocted in her mind. This realization brought a feeling of temporary relief and resolve to Catherine's mind. This surely would be enough to convince Dr. Thomas to let her out of the hospital. Life would go on as normal. If she had any more images of the calendar house, she would simply dismiss them. The wooden house was gone and the images would eventually leave too, Catherine was convinced of that. It wasn't long before Dr. Thomas showed up at her bedside.

"How are you feeling today, Catherine?" Dr. Thomas inquired.

"I feel much better. I am really convinced that it is all in my mind and it has always been in my mind. Last night I was frightened by it, but today, I feel so calm about it. I feel so much better that I think I want to return back to my life and go on as before," Catherine answered in an assuring voice. Her countenance and demeanor impressed Dr. Thomas.

"I think the new medication is starting to have a good effect upon you. It's always a process of adjustment with trial and error to find the right combination of medications that fit your needs. I was quite concerned about your out of control behavior yesterday. Are you sure that you don't feel the same?"

"I feel more peaceful and I think I would feel okay even if I wasn't somewhat sedated. Thinking about what happened yesterday really convinced me it's just like you said-totally concocted in my mind. That image was totally in my mind! It wasn't *real*. And that's okay. It's okay. Don't you think?" Catherine answered earnestly.

"It will be okay as long as you keep things like this straight in your mind. That's up to you, Catherine, and it's your challenge. You have one amazing imagination I believe. Maybe you should take up writing. It might do you some good to share these ideas with others," Dr. Thomas suggested.

"I don't like to write. But maybe I will try to write something down one of these days. Dr. Thomas, do you think I can get out of here soon? I don't feel like ending my life anymore. I do want to live. I felt so hopeless but now I feel better. I really mean that. I just want to go home and get back to my job. I need to work. Work helps keep me sane. You know that. Will you please let me go home, today perhaps?" Catherine begged.

"We'll see," Dr. Thomas said, patting her hand softly, "we just have to make sure that you are okay when the sedatives wear off. Why don't you get dressed and walk around a bit when you feel up to it. There's a therapy room where you can go do a puzzle or play a game if you'd like."

"Okay. I think I would like that. I still feel a little out of it so I will wait a bit," Catherine replied.

Later that afternoon, Catherine found herself engrossed in a crossword puzzle book. She enjoyed herself when she worked on these and found the puzzles quite easy. This lifted her spirits even further and she felt more hopeful about being released soon. She looked around at the two other patients sitting in the easy chairs, watching television. Catherine wondered what ailment brought them to this mental hospital. Did they have challenges with discerning reality or the desire to end their life too? Catherine thought about saying something to them but decided to keep silent and refocus on the puzzle.

Once upon a time, Catherine could never have imagined herself in such an institution. The only time she ever went to such a place is when she accompanied her mother to visit a friend. The place frightened her but she never shared her feelings with her mother. As a child, she didn't share feelings easily. When she met

James, she was quite shy, but he had a great effect on her personality and she was able to overcome a lot of her shyness. After losing her wonderful companion, she just resumed many of her former personality traits. Now the thought of speaking to people just repelled her and she preferred to quietly remain to herself.

As Catherine finished up the crossword puzzle, her thoughts wandered back to her present reality. Life had brought Catherine tremendous trials, perhaps mightier than most people would ever face, and here she was, struggling to stay sane. Could she keep a grip on this thin thread of reality she had formulated in her brain to convince the doctor and herself that she could go on and survive?

"I just have to focus on getting out of here," Catherine thought as she glanced at the clock hanging on the wall. The day was getting late and she could see that it had finally stopped snowing looking out the windowpane in the room. The sun was coming out. The sunlight was a welcome sight. She looked around the room and noticed the several Christmas decorations placed here and there on the walls. They appeared to be quite old and faded. The reminder of the coming holiday caused her heart to drop. The feelings of excitement and anticipation that accompany the days before Christmas for most people were now completely absent in Catherine. She sighed. She drummed her fingers nervously on the table and decided she had enough of the room and crossword puzzles for the time being.

Catherine walked slowly back to her room. She didn't want to spend one more night in this place and hoped with all her might she might find Dr. Thomas willing to sign her release. She no longer felt the effects of the sedatives. She still felt okay. Her resolve about her "problem" seemed to be intact. She had lost those feelings of hopelessness. Catherine was so grateful to once again have been able to climb out of the dark abyss of despair. It was like a monster with tentacles that lurked at the bottom that was constantly was seeking to pull Catherine back down. The new medicine seemed to be helping her.

When she came back to her room, a rather large black man with a beaming smile greeted her, delivering her dinner.

"Good afternoon, how are you doing this fine day?" he asked.

"I'm fine," she answered quietly.

"My name is Maurice. What's yours?"

"Catherine."

"Catherine is a pretty name for a lovely lady. I'm here to deliver you this fine dinner, compliments of the hospital cafeteria chef."

Catherine groaned.

"I'll be sure to tell him that!" Maurice responded with a chuckle. He started to whistle a familiar Christmas tune, "We wish you a Merry Christmas" as he left her room, and beamed her another big smile.

She looked down at the typical institutional meal and sighed. The food was probably one of the worst things about her stay. She didn't like food too much to begin with and this hospital food was for the most part, hard for her to swallow. Yesterday, the stew she ordered was awful. Soup was usually a safe bet so that is what she ordered today. She sipped the soup and munched on a cracker. The soup didn't taste too bad today but she just wanted to be home eating her own food in her own kitchen. Catherine thought about her dismal little house and what a contrast it was to her once charming home full of merriment, love and life. The home she had with James shimmered with a special luster that is only found within the walls of a home where family time is cherished and relationships are nourished. Catherine tried with all her might to end this reminiscing at once as it began to wear away at her resolve to be strong as she once again faced Dr. Thomas.

He came into her a few minutes later and sat down in the chair by her bed. He was writing on a clipboard before he said anything to Catherine. She stared quietly at him, trying to gather her thoughts.

"I think you have made sufficient progress today that I think you might be able to go home this evening. I'm not completely comfortable with discharging you yet but I know how anxious you are to get back to your life," Dr. Thomas said finally.

Catherine sighed with relief. "Thank you, Dr. Thomas. I am so glad to hear that. I feel better and better and I am ready to put all of this behind me."

"If you have any problems, I will be available to help. Just give me a call. It might be harder for you once you get home. If I recall, you always seem to have a much harder time of things right before Christmas. It's already the seventh of December so Christmas is not far away. I worry that you will not be able to handle it very well this year. You need to find something that will take your mind off your loneliness," Dr. Thomas responded, thought for a moment and then suggested, "perhaps you might consider spending time helping at, say, a food kitchen or some other benevolent cause? It would help take the focus off you and your situation. It can be quite therapeutic."

"Maybe I will," Catherine answered. That is what she always said to him when he offered her suggestions to help her deal with things better.

"Well, it's only a suggestion but I have had good experiences doing that sort of thing this time of year. It seems to always lighten my heart. My wife got me to try it one year. I enjoyed it and ever since we have made it a yearly tradition. Every year we look for such opportunities. There is always some cause that needs our help," Dr. Thomas suggested with added enthusiasm in his voice.

Catherine thought about a time her parents had taken her and Tina to help at a church that was making some kind of relief boxes that contained some Christmas items, food, clothing and toys to give to poor people. She did remember feeling happy there. It was a good memory. She began to think about her parents and renewed sad feelings returned. Maybe she would try to call them after she got home. Catherine felt nervous once again and decided the time wasn't right yet to call.

Before long, Catherine was trudging through the deep snow in an effort to find her buried car in the parking lot that looked like a sparkling winter wonderland in the twilight. She became quite exasperated. It was bitter cold and the sky was crystal clear. The bright moon was coming up on the horizon and a few stars twinkled in the darkening sky. After what seemed to be an eternity, she recognized her vehicle with high mounds of snow piled on top. It seemed to have more snow on it than any other car. Her gloves failed to keep her fingers warm as she attempted to sweep the thick pile of fluffy ice crystals off the windshield. She glanced at the hospital as she slowly edged out of the parking lot, feeling grateful for her freedom and hoping for clearer road conditions on the way home.

After a long, arduous and scary journey, she pulled into the driveway and sighed with relief. She noticed something in front of her door that was partly covered by snow. At once, thoughts of the mysterious package found there seven days ago returned. Gathering her courage, she left her car and approached the door. As Catherine glanced down at the item, it looked immediately familiar. It was the calendar house! Seven little windows glowed brightly through the covering of snow. Catherine gasped. She quickly opened the door, entered her home, slammed the door, turned on the light and sat sown in her recliner. She was in a panic. That house was only in her imagination. Catherine told herself that she had just imagined seeing it on her doorway, just like she had a week ago. Dr. Thomas had physically removed the wood from her possession. The last thing he would ever do was to return it to her at her house. "The delusion is persisting and I have got to figure out what to do about it", thought Catherine.

Catherine sat paralyzed by her fear for a long time. She longed to be back within the safety of the mental hospital because she felt stronger there. Catherine began to drift off to sleep in the darkness. Another dream came upon her. This time it was even more strange and eerie. She was running from something, but she didn't know what. It was dark in this dream, so dark that she couldn't see anything. She thought she might be in a tunnel.

Then she saw something up ahead of her. It was a man. He was calling to her. As she ran to escape what was behind her, she suddenly recognized the face of the man. It was her dead husband, James! He looked the same as she remembered him. He had sandy brown hair, dark brown eyes and dimples when he smiled. He spoke in a sweet persuasive voice that seemed to melt Catherine's heart when she heard his words, "Look darling, and see."

Suddenly Catherine awoke, again startled by the reality of the dream and how it made her feel. Catherine felt a mixture of immense anguish from the scariness of the dream and overwhelming joy at seeing the face of her sweetheart again. Tears welled up and dropped from her eyes. It had been so long since she had seen his face and heard his kind voice. She was very frightened from having another realistic dream. She had just barely gone to sleep when it came upon her. She wished for some more of the strong sleep medication so she could avoid seeing these troubling surreal scenes of her loved ones. Then she thought about the words James had spoken to her.

"Could he have meant the house? But it's just a figment of my imagination! Oh, why is this happening to me?" Catherine cried out loud in the darkness as she began to sob again. After a long time, once the hot bitter tears ebbed, she was seized by the desire to grab the house once again to look and see. She quickly opened the door, reached down and grabbed the house. It was extremely cold outside so Catherine immediately came back inside. With her hands nervously shaking, she brushed off the snow and looked at the seventh window now lit.

# December 8th

Catherine couldn't get the image of the seventh window out of her mind the next morning. She had a terrible night of sleep. The image haunted her sleep and nightmarish compilations of her current reality and bits and pieces of her past swirled anxiously in her mind on and off during the night. She even considered calling Dr. Thomas in the middle of the night in her anguish. She wanted to get her hands on some more of that sleep medication she was given in the hospital. She longed for peace. She yearned for solace of mind. She looked at the bottles of sleep medication in her medicine cabinet and grabbed a few pills. As much as Catherine wished for some relief, the nagging fear of returning to the hospital kept her from telling Dr. Thomas anything.

There simply had to be a logical explanation for everything that was happening. Was someone playing a terrible trick on her? Catherine's mind reviewed the short list of people she could recall that knew her well enough to even consider such a stunt. That seemed to take her nowhere. She turned on the television set, hoping for a distracting movie but all she found was stupid infomercials and late night talk shows. Catherine searched for her latest novel. She tried to read it but she couldn't seem to focus. Catherine couldn't seem to escape the persistent image of the seventh window. She eventually drifted off to sleep and found some relief for a time.

Now Catherine was wide-awake as she looked at the alarm clock beside her bed. It was still dark but the clock indicated it was time to get up for work. As much as she wanted to return to work for a piece of sanity because work always provided a respite from her dull, pathetic and painful existence, she worried about the day ahead of her. She was grateful to have such a mind for accounting but now she doubted even work would bring her emotional rest. The seventh image seemed to cut to her heart more than any other of the preceding images. Perhaps it was because it reminded her of the sweetest and most wonderful memory of her life. Normally the most cherished memories of life bring joy to even the most downcast of hearts, but for poor Catherine, the opposite was the case. The memories resurrected by last night's image were like a stab to her feeble heart.

Catherine was a junior in college when a group of her friends decided to go to a nearby town for a Christmas festival right before finals. Catherine tried to talk her way out of it because she wasn't feeling comfortable about one upcoming final. Her friends persisted and convinced her that it would be a blast and help her relax for her test that following Monday. She reluctantly agreed to go. It turned out to be a truly magical night. The town was beautifully decorated for the season, which really complimented its normal appearance. It was an exquisite town to behold with old Victorian styled homes and well-manicured yards. The center of town was well kept, clean and had a particular charm of its own with many old fashioned buildings with interesting classic embellishments.

Cheerful colored lights that adorned the charming structures, softened by gently falling snow in the crisp night air, created a very memorable setting. It was an outdoor celebration in the center of town accompanied by jolly Christmas music, hot chocolate and carnival like food vendors offering delectable holiday treats, bonfires to help warm nippy fingers, and free ice skating. The town was alive with excitement and merriment. Long lines of delighted children waited to visit Santa Claus who had ridden into town on a beautifully decorated float during the Christmas parade at sundown. Catherine was in awe at the scene. It reminded her of a fairy tale setting or even what a child might imagine Santa Claus's North Pole to be like. It brought out the child in everyone present.

The ice rink was located in the city park next to a large white gazebo. The old-fashioned structure was adorned with sparkling white lights and colorful holiday wreaths. For years during the summer, the gazebo had been an enjoyable little dancehall. Now holiday music piped over the speakers provided enough incentive to lure some older couples to gaily dance. The gazebo was a captivating centerpiece to the evening's celebrations.

Catherine and her girlfriends giggled excitedly like little schoolgirls as they awkwardly skated on wobbly ankles grabbing each other's arms for stability. It was quite a comical sight. There seemed to be quite an assortment of young men gathered in huddles on the side of the skating rink that seemed to take notice of the entourage of amateur female skaters. The occasional excited screams from the girls really piqued the young men's interest in pursuing contact with the joyful ladies. Some of Catherine's friends began to notice the interest of the bystanders and decided to plan a sudden spill to see what might happen. Catherine was oblivious to their plans as she did her best to focus at steadying her feet. She had only skated once before in her life and managed to wipe out pretty bad at that time so she was quite hesitant about repeating the experience.

Catherine had dated very little in both high school and college. She was attractive but very shy. As she grabbed her girlfriend's arm to get help steadying her shaky legs, out of the corner of her eye she noticed an agreeable looking fellow giving her an attentive gaze. For a moment she managed a grin before she found herself suddenly atop a pile of giggling girls scattered about the ice. The spill had occurred so quickly she didn't even feel herself fall. Fortunately the bodies beneath her cushioned the blow this time.

A gentle hand reached down to pull Catherine up. It was the young gentleman who had just caught Catherine's eye as she tumbled. She gazed up at his pleasant face. Her hand felt warm in his as she grasped it. His warm smile brightened as she held his hand as if he felt the special warmth suddenly too. It was a moment never to be forgotten by either party. Undeniably, something stirred in their hearts.

Catherine felt an excitement she never felt before and at the same time, hesitation. Who was this young man? James Daley resisted any hesitation and firmly pulled Catherine up off the ice. As soon as she stood upright, he began to pull her gently away from the heap of girls still giggling on the ice. Catherine did not let go but held his hand as tight as she could. The couple slowly skated in silence around the ice rink, amazed at what they were individually feeling.

James could endure the silence no longer and interrupted with, "I'm James Daley," Catherine quietly answered back, "I'm Catherine Jensen." The silence resumed and after another long pause around the rink, James asked sincerely, "Did that fall hurt you, Catherine?" She softly chuckled and answered with a soft "no".

The couple seemed completely comfortable together gliding along the smooth ice that was dusted with a layer of fresh sparkling snow. The tightly joined hands felt magically connected. Catherine seemed to lose her awkwardness on the ice with James's steady skating guiding her. Catherine felt her heart pounding within her with the excitement she was feeling for the first time in her life. She had met her true love.

Catherine wiped away the bittersweet tears as she thought once more about the image in the seventh window, which displayed the ice-skating rink and the brightly lit gazebo from that charming holiday celebration so long ago. She missed her true love more than ever and the pain it created in her heart was more than she could endure. Feelings of hopelessness began to resurface and Catherine began to panic. She had to get a grip on her feelings. It was time to get ready for work.

It had been a long week. The stress from everything that happened was taking a serious toll on Catherine's wellbeing. However, with the resolve that still lingered in her mind, she would have a successful return to work. She refused to look at the calendar as she prepared for work. As anguish began to well in her mind, she did her best to force it out. It was the greatest struggle she ever endured. The reality of her sadness and loneliness was now front and center in her life but Catherine hoped to escape to work for some solace from her pain.

The presence of snow on the road added an agonizing challenge in driving to work. It was even more terrorizing than the previous night's excursion home due to a lot of traffic and near misses on the slippery roads. Catherine avoided her co-workers as best she could when they saw her that morning. Catherine's face showed obvious signs of emotional wear and tear. If there were rumors circulating about her, she wanted to make sure she spoke to no one except her boss, Frank Barton. He was the only one that knew of her recent stay in the mental hospital. He was very relieved to see her immediate return to work as she was one of his best employees but at the same time, harbored worries about her mental stability and how it might negatively affect her work performance.

Just before lunch, Alice appeared in her doorway with a small wrapped gift.

"I made you this. I hope you're doing okay. I have been very worried about you."

Catherine looked up surprised at her co-worker. She thanked Alice quietly for the gift. She opened the gift, which was a knitted scarf in a soft color of pink.

"It's very pretty. I needed a scarf like this. Thank you for thinking about me," Catherine responded.

"I love to knit. It is stress reliever for me and I have been making plenty of them for gifts this year. Would you like to join me for lunch today?"

This offering of friendship from Alice made her feel uncomfortable and awkward about how to respond next. She did not want to spend any time with Alice where she might divulge any information about her situation. Alice was concerned but also curious what was going on with Catherine and she did not want this nosey woman asking her questions. She declined the offer for lunch by stating she was anxious about her deadlines and the need to complete overdue assignments. Alice sensed her uneasiness and graciously left her alone.

As the day wore on, Catherine found it increasingly difficult to remain firm in her resolve to not dwell on any thoughts about the most recent Christmas scene from the calendar house. The cracks in her emotional dam were growing. Several times she slipped away to the women's room to cry, each time feeling more out of control emotionally than before. She worried about the looks her boss was giving her as he passed by her office more frequently than usual. She had completed an important report that was a little overdue to Frank in the morning and felt relieved that the work was finally off her desk. Several times he paused as if he wanted to say something, but then continued on his way. This only made Catherine feel more anxious.

Working with numbers, which had always managed to keep Catherine's mind occupied, now seemed irrelevant and distracting to her. This had never happened before at her job. A new fear began to surface in her mind. Catherine was now faced with the reality that she was losing all grip on her small manageable life that she had established, which insulated her emotionally for a long time. She had found some solace from her miserable existence showing up to work each day and digging into numbers with some satisfaction, but now Catherine just felt empty inside. She had built a wall around herself and her job only required minimal interaction with the world of people around her. All the people that really mattered to her at all were just faded memories and terrible heartaches.

Things went from bad to worse by the end of the day when Frank Barton appeared in her doorway and requested a meeting with her first thing the next morning. Catherine sensed this would not be a pleasant meeting with him because of his demeanor and when he mentioned the report she had turned in earlier. She did her best to respond professionally to him as she gathered up her things to leave.  She dreaded going home once again, especially after the long day, so she opted for dinner and a movie at the local mall.  The movie succeeded in keeping her mind occupied for a few hours but when she got home, a flood of worry and grief completely overwhelmed her.  She glanced at the beautiful calendar house by the door in her living room, brighter with one more window lit.  Catherine reached down and grabbed it, shook the house angrily out of pure frustration before she peered into the 8th window.  Immediately the scene inside took her back to the magical time of her wedding.

Catherine and James had decided to get married before Christmas.  James had just graduated from college and was planning on entering graduate school in January.  They had dated for a year while they attended college in neighboring cities.  They saw each other on the weekends.  James had planned on marrying Catherine shortly after their meeting on the ice rink. He fell in love with her immediately but he promised his parents he would graduate before getting married.  James waited until the right moment to ask Catherine.  They had decided to take a short trip to visit the magical little town where they first met.

As New England towns go, it was as quaint as they come, and an enjoyable get-away any time of year.  It happened to be that magical time when the deciduous trees put on their amazing show of color.  The feel of cool crisp air and the sight of blazing leaves in the sunshine amidst the picturesque town created a wonderful autumn setting. The couple reminisced as they strolled around the park and walked into the white gazebo. James quietly brought out a small diamond ring and gently placed it on Catherine's finger. She answered yes to his sweet simple question of marriage. It was a precious moment.

Catherine was so excited to plan her wedding even if it was the busiest time of the year and most of the details for the wedding were done right after finals. They got married in a delightful little church and the reception hall was beautifully decorated with wreaths of dark green fir adorned with red roses and baby's breath and little white Christmas lights. The wedding scene shining brightly in the little window was so beautiful to Catherine that it took her breath away. Such was the memorable wedding day of Catherine and James Daley as they started their lives together.

# *December 9ᵗʰ*

It was another agonizing night of sleep for poor Catherine. Now she couldn't get the memories of her engagement, sweet wedding and honeymoon out of her mind no matter how hard she tried. She simply gave up, stopped fighting and let the thoughts flow freely, which only stirred the very deepest of emotions in her heart and added to her growing anguish. It was almost like watching a movie about her life because she seemed to recall and visualize with amazing detail the sequence of events of that first year with James, which led to their becoming husband and wife. Pondering on the images she recalled only increased her longing for the sweet companionship she had with her first and only true love.

After their first meeting on the ice skating rink, Catherine and James seemed to be oblivious to their other friends who now noticed the spark of chemistry between the young co-eds. The couple spent the remainder of the evening together on the ice skating rink and then strolled around the festivities until Catherine was forced away by her friends to return home. James and Catherine had talked some and shared phone numbers but mostly they just enjoyed holding hands and feeling marvelous together amidst a magical winter wonderland. As this memory captured her thoughts, for a moment Catherine experienced that special emotional sensation she felt so wonderfully many years before.

"I really had it perfect for a while," Catherine said quietly in the dark. The Christmas holiday was quickly approaching and all Catherine wanted to do was stay in the past with her thoughts and dwell on the time when Christmas was magical and joyful. Her memory was alert and the feelings triggered were sweet. She never wanted to go back to reality again. The alarm clock rudely brought Catherine back to the truth. Catherine sighed as the comforting bubble she seemed to be floating in suddenly burst. It was time to get ready for work. A nagging feeling of worry returned to her mind.

"What does Frank want to see me about?" Catherine wondered as she readied herself for work, "Yesterday was terrible." Catherine shook her head as she recalled how poorly she performed at work on the simplest of tasks. She suddenly realized that she never double-checked the report before giving it to her boss. Catherine always made a huge effort to review her work and make sure things looked perfect.

"I can't imagine myself not doing any checking. Oh, what's wrong with me? I know that report was extremely important and it was already delayed because of my absence. I really am losing my mind." Catherine felt so disappointed in herself. Her work performance was one thing she felt good about in her life and now she felt she had sabotaged her reputation.

Catherine skipped breakfast as she hurried to the office early. Her stomach was in a knot. She sat in her car nervously pondering what she might say to her boss. When she could stand it no more, she struggled out the car door and walked slowly to her office. She looked over the report on her desk and felt her face flush as she read the comments written on post it notes. She had made a number of mistakes. It was an agonizing moment for Catherine. Tears welled up in her eyes. She shook her head in disgust and walked slowly to Frank Barton's office down the hall feeling like a schoolchild on the way to the principal's office.

Frank Barton had been owner of Precise Accounting Services for many years. He prided himself on providing accuracy above all else. He simply looked down on anyone who displayed weakness of any kind, especially emotional weakness. Catherine had always performed to his standard and always acted professionally up until now. He looked the part of an aging businessman who had spent many long hours at the office. His baldhead had just a few tufts of brownish gray hair on the side and back. Thick lenses shielded his dark brown eyes. Today, those eyes looked even darker to Catherine.

Frank looked up at Catherine as she entered the room and asked her to have a seat and close the door behind her. He wasn't smiling. Catherine obeyed. She looked nervously around the room waiting for him to speak again.

"Catherine, did you get a chance to look at the report I left on your desk?" Frank inquired.

Catherine only nodded, looking down at the floor.

"I'm so sorry," Catherine replied softly.

"It was very surprising to see this quality of work from you. You have been such a great employee and one I could always count on for accuracy. That report was extremely important. If I hadn't checked it myself and found all those errors, the results could have been disastrous. I realize you just had a stay in the hospital and perhaps we can attribute this performance to your mental state, which I can only imagine is still questionable," Frank pointed out in a cold tone of voice that surprised Catherine. She had always enjoyed a good working relationship with him in the past. She was now seeing another side of him that scared her. She didn't know how to respond so she sat quietly.

"Perhaps you can explain why your behavior has suddenly changed. I noticed this even before your stay at the mental hospital. You are acting in a most unprofessional way. You work performance yesterday was quite frankly, unacceptable. There must be a reason for this," Frank demanded.

Catherine fought back the tears as best she could realizing that Frank's harsh disapproval of her behavior would only get worse as her emotional state weakened. Her silence prompted even more demands from Frank.

"Catherine, I need to know what is going on with you and what has triggered this decline. You must tell me!"

Catherine wasn't sure how to respond without sounding completely crazy. It was so awkward. She hesitated to answer, looking up at Frank occasionally but mostly looking down as she nervously wrung her hands together.

The silence became unbearable for Frank who then said, "If you don't tell me, I will have to take drastic measures with you!"

Catherine knew her job was on the line either way so she sighed and then answered quietly, "What I am about to tell you will sound very strange, but it is all true. It all began about nine days ago when I came home from work. I found an interesting looking package on my doorstep. When I opened it, I was surprised to find a carved wooden house that had twenty-four little windows on it. The window with a golden number one on it was lit up and it showed a scene from my childhood. Each day another window was lit up showing a different scene from my past. I don't know who sent it, why I found it or how it works or anything. It's reminded me of some wonderful things that occurred in my life but it is also a terrible reminder of my personal tragedy in losing the family I loved so many years ago. I am trying to deal with this, but it's been very hard."

Frank looked at Catherine with dismay, his dark eyes flaring.

"You're trying to tell me that you're falling to pieces because someone sent you a package? This doesn't make any sense!" Frank roared, "What you're saying is simply impossible. You're just making this up but I don't understand why. Why, Catherine?"

"I'm not making this up," Catherine responded indignantly, "it is true. It's at my house right now."

Frank refused to hear another word as he nervously got up from his desk and paced back and forth for a minute or so.

"I can't have you working at the office. You will take a leave of absence starting immediately. You must get a handle on your mental illness. You're delusional. I know this seems harsh but I think it's in your and the company's best interest. You may return when you are well," Frank added.

Catherine was stunned.

"Are you letting me go if I don't get better?" Catherine asked, looking dismayed at Frank. She felt shocked and very angry at his treatment of her. She didn't bring this upon herself. She didn't ask for the package to show up on her doorstep. Now she was probably going to lose her job because of it. Frank was convinced she was crazy.

"No, but if you don't get better soon, we will make this a permanent solution. I cannot have such an employee in my company. Please remove your things, go home and contact your doctor. I don't why he let you out of that hospital so soon!" Frank barked.

Catherine got up angrily and with all the emotion she could muster turned to face Frank.

"Mr. Barton, I have been an excellent employee for you for many years. I have always been on time and I have always produced accurate work on time. Your treatment of me today is horrible and I do not deserve it! I didn't ask for this to happen to me but it did. I didn't ask for my family to be killed in a car wreck but it happened. I know I am having some very severe emotional challenges right now but how can you be so cruel to me?" Catherine sobbed.

"I cannot have an employee in my midst that cannot control her emotions. It is simply not tolerated here. This is an office of professionals. You are a sick woman. Get a grip or else!" Frank responded.

"It's not right! It's not right!" Catherine screamed as she left his office creating quite a stir among the normally quiet working environment. Employees stood up in their cubicles to view the disturbance. This public display of emotional weakness from Catherine troubled Frank Barton even further and he quickly closed the door as she departed.

"The sooner she's out of here the better. What a disgraceful woman! I can't believe she would act that way in front of everyone, probably did it just to embarrass me. What a pity to lose such a fine employee but I simply cannot have her here in this emotional state anymore. She's lost her mind," Frank muttered to himself as he sat down in the office chair and rubbed his troubled forehead. A vague feeling of guilt settled over him but was quickly dismissed as he picked up the ringing telephone.

Catherine ran, grabbed her things as quickly as possible and headed to her car. She sobbed and sobbed. She sat in her car not knowing what to do next.

Her refuge of emotional safety was suddenly gone. Her job had kept her sane. It had kept her going. It had allowed her to live a simple, safe and emotionally insulated life for a long time. What would she do now? Should she check back into that dreadful hospital? Should she call Dr. Thomas? Should she just go home and deal with things there?  That calendar house would be waiting for her, shining brightly with scenes from her past, providing further torment to her anguished soul.

Catherine was getting cold.  It was time to act.  She forced herself to drive home down the slippery roads, ignoring the Christmas decorations hanging over the streets partially covered by snow, and the Christmas shoppers loaded up with packages among the downtown shops.

It was strange to be home at such an early hour of the day. The house seemed unusually dismal to her now.  It certainly wasn't a place she could go to feel happier.  It was dreary.  She noticed her answering machine was flashing.  There were three messages from Dr. Thomas asking Catherine to call him.  Catherine remembered she was supposed to call him to let him know how things were going so far.  She didn't feel like talking to anyone, especially Dr. Thomas right now.  She grabbed the cord and yanked it out of the wall. She looked around in the tiny kitchen and her eyes focused on the mysterious calendar house sitting on her kitchen counter.  She had failed to notice it earlier in her rush to get out of the house and off to work.

Now the window for day nine was brightly glowing.  She sighed deeply.  Catherine sadly walked over to pick it up.  She peered into the little window and saw a small little Christmas tree with homemade ornaments and hand baked gingerbread men adorning it. Immediately she recalled her first Christmas as James's wife. They were very poor as most graduate students are. Catherine did her best to decorate their little apartment with simple items. The newlyweds tried to focus on giving rather than getting so the true spirit of Christmas was present in their hearts. It was very special to her because of the feelings of Christmas joy that filled their little home.

Oh how Catherine longed for that time again. She longed to be with her true love. She yearned to hold her children again and kiss them. Catherine wept as she never had before and inside she felt completely empty. That calendar house was a curse. All it did was dredge up memories. It couldn't bring these loved ones back. It was a cruel hoax. The calendar house had pushed her to the brink and she was done.

"I will never have joy again. It's just no use. I live a horrible existence. Why am I still here? There's no point to my life now," Catherine moaned. Feeling hopeless, she went to her bedroom still holding onto the wooden house.

As the day wore on, Catherine laid in her bed trying to read in an effort to prevent her depression from worsening. It wasn't working. She thought about calling Dr. Thomas but realized he really wasn't helping her deal with her problem when he couldn't even see her problem. She would do without his help this time. The bleakest of thoughts were dominating her mind. Her hope of a better day was fading quickly. There was no point to her tomorrow. Satisfaction at her job was now a thing of the past. Life offered nothing. It was a mental tug of war between light and dark. The darkness was winning.

By late evening, when she could tolerate consciousness no more, she got up and went to her bathroom cabinet. Catherine desperately grabbed the almost full bottle of sleeping pills and took it back to her bedside. She swallowed two pills and put the bottle back on her nightstand. Catherine hesitated for a moment but then grabbed the bottle again and poured out the entire contents into her palm.

# *December 10th*

Dr. Thomas had tried to reach Catherine at her home the previous day with no luck. Her answering machine had picked up his calls initially but then the phone just rang and rang. Dr. Thomas sensed something was terribly wrong. It was getting very late in the day and thought he might be able to reach Catherine at her employer. He left several messages on her office phone. She wasn't at her office either. Now Dr. Thomas was very worried, as she did not seem to be following the agreed upon protocol of checking in with him from time to time so he could chart her progress.

Dr. Thomas decided then to check to see if anyone knew her whereabouts at work so he looked up the number for Precise Accounting Services. It was after hours but soon he was on the phone with Frank Barton who tended to stay at work late most evenings. After inquiring about Catherine Daley's whereabouts, Dr. Thomas sensed Frank Barton was quite upset with Catherine. He kept insisting that his employees must follow a code of conduct and performance and that Catherine upon returning to work had failed to behave in a professional way. Frank also reprimanded Dr. Thomas for letting his patient out of the mental hospital prematurely. He also mentioned something about a little wooden house that was dropped at her doorstep and that she imagined it showed pictures of her past in tiny little windows and Catherine said it was in her house right now. After hearing that story, Frank was convinced that Catherine had gone completely crazy and that it was a good thing that she had been sent home on indefinite leave.

Upon hearing this, Dr. Thomas asked when Catherine was sent home. He was overcome with worry, as she had been sent home early in the day, obviously very distraught and unpredictable. He also wondered how Catherine managed to get her hands back on that piece of wood as it had been removed physically from the hospital. Dr. Thomas ended the phone conversation with a reprimand to Frank and told him that despite Catherine's current behavior, his insensitive treatment of a good employee would come back to haunt him and the reputation of his company would suffer and that he should be ashamed of himself.

Frank slammed down the phone when he heard Dr. Thomas's remarks. Later, Frank had a terrible night of sleep.

Dr. Thomas decided it was time to go home from his office. He dialed Catherine's home phone once again with no luck. He decided to drive over to the address listed in her chart and see if she was home. It was getting late and Dr. Thomas was hungry for dinner. He called his wife about his plans and headed over to Catherine's residence. To Dr. Thomas's dismay, no one was home. No one answered the door and no lights were on. He trudged through the deep snow and tried to peer inside but didn't see anything in any of the windows. The house seemed vacant. He decided to venture over to a neighbor's house to inquire if the neighbor had seen any evidence of Catherine that day or evening. Unfortunately, the man had no idea what he was talking about and made it seem that no one lived in that house anymore. It hadn't been rented for some time. Dr. Thomas was puzzled and then quite upset that he didn't have her correct address on his records. That seemed quite odd. Discouraged, Dr. Thomas went home.

Later that night, Carol Jones returned home after an evening college class and found her husband John dozing on the couch. She hesitated to wake him up but she then remembered how mad he would be in the morning if he slept there all night.

"Honey, you better wake up now or the couch will be your curse in the morning," Carol yelled as her husband quickly opened his eyes at the reminder. He sat up swiftly and asked, "How was your class?"

"It was fun. I love art classes. I don't know why it took me so long to start doing art. Maybe just your encouragement was all I needed. I should have met you years ago," Carol answered as she leaned over and kissed her husband on the forehead, "what did you do tonight?"

"I watched a movie and the end of a football game on TV. Oh yeah. Some guy came by asking about the house across the street and if some lady lived there. I don't know whom he was talking about. It seems like that house has been empty as long as I have lived here."

Carol thought a moment and then said, "It has been empty for a long time hasn't it? I wonder if he was looking for Catherine."

"Who's Catherine?" John asked.

"Oh, a lady who lived in that house a while back and then suddenly moved out not telling me where she went to. I helped save her life once when she overdosed on some pills. I hope she's okay," Carol answered.

"Wow, you saved her life? You never told me about that. What happened?"

"It's been a number of years, a long time before we met. I hardly knew her at the time. She was one to really keep to herself.

One night I was falling asleep when suddenly I had the most vivid dream. It scared me half to death and I woke up immediately. I'd just seen Catherine in my dream and she was trying to kill herself by overdosing on some medication. I couldn't stop thinking about her and worrying so I dragged myself out of bed and went over to see how she was. Nobody answered the front door so I went snooping around the back. Fortunately she had left the back door open and sure enough, when I found her in bed, she was unconscious with an empty medicine bottle beside her bed. I called 911 and waited for the ambulance to show. She somehow made it and was in a hospital for some time. It's strange how I would have such a dream, and so vivid too, that I felt the urgency to check on her. I wonder if she's still alive. I don't even know that much about her. I tried to get to know her a bit when she returned home from the hospital but it wasn't long and she packed up and moved away. I wonder if she's still in town."

"That's some story!" John declared as he got up off the couch and hugged his wife.

"Tell me more about this guy who came to the door asking about her," Carol requested, suddenly feeling a deep concern again for Catherine, similar to what she had felt years ago.

"The man seemed pretty upset and very worried. He looked like a doctor I thought. I think he was wearing some kind of medical badge," John added.

"I wished I knew where she lived now. I am really feeling concern for her wellbeing, just like I did before. It's such a strange feeling. I hope she didn't try to kill herself again!"

"I wonder why she moved away from you after you helped save her life. She sounds like a lady with lots of problems," John commented. "It's getting late, let's go to bed," Carol agreed.

Later that night, Carol woke up. She hadn't had any dreams she could remember for a long time but now she sat pondering over the vivid dream she just woke up from.

"That was so real! It's like I was walking in my dream. That street looked so familiar to me, like it's a street here in town, but I'm not sure. Why did I pause so long at that one house? I can even remember the address. It is 944 Sycamore," Carol thought to herself in the darkness. Suddenly she understood, turned on the bedside lamp, grabbed a piece of paper and wrote down the address. At once, she thought of Catherine. Perhaps this was her new residence or just a crazy coincidence. She had to find out. Carol went to the kitchen and found the phone book. She located a Sycamore Street on the map and got dressed. Her husband managed to wake up.

"What are you doing Carol? It is 3:00 AM," John asked, "why are you getting dressed?"

"You're not going to believe this John, but I just had a really vivid dream. It was really weird. I was walking in my dream and I was on a street that looked kind of familiar to me and then I came to this small house and stood there and stared at it for the longest time. Then I woke up. Isn't that strange? What's even stranger is that I remember seeing the address! I wrote it down here on this paper. The address is 944 Sycamore, and there is a Sycamore street in town. I just looked it up on the phone book map. I have to go check it out. I feel very worried like I did before for Catherine. I know she doesn't want anything to do with me but I feel like I have to do this. Maybe this is her address and I have some bizarre ability to help her through these dreams of mine. I don't know what to think. I really don't want to get involved with her again but I just feel compelled. I know I won't be able to go back to sleep until I check this all out. You need to go back to sleep. I'll be fine. I won't be long," Carol reassured her sleepy husband.

Catherine lay in her bed as she faded in and out of consciousness. Her decision to take all of the pills had come only a few minutes earlier. Now she lay quietly in her bed, waiting for her final night of sleep. She had chosen to make a quiet exit out of a pathetic life. It would be a simple funeral. Perhaps her family would come and a few sympathetic co-workers who knew bits and pieces of her life and say goodbye. It didn't matter now. The calendar house didn't matter now. It glowed at her from across the bedroom floor. When she went to look at it for the last time, the tenth window lit up brightly with another heart wrenching scene. Catherine saw a little teddy bear with a cute Santa Claus hat on it nestled in a soft pink baby blanket. She immediately pictured in her mind her darling newborn daughter, snuggled up warm in the blanket. She had been born a few weeks before Christmas and one of her baby gifts was the little Santa Claus teddy bear. Her firstborn daughter Susie had been a delightful child.

Catherine couldn't stand the pain a minute longer. A wretched drunk driver had yanked her precious children from her loving arms. She thought over and over again," Why my babies? Why my sweetheart? Why do I have to have this torturous house? Why doesn't it just disappear? Why do I have to recall all of this? I don't have them any longer and never will again." The images and memories it displayed made her hate her present life more than ever. She couldn't go back to when her life was good. Catherine felt she had no more to offer. She was insane, trapped in a dark little world, surrounded by guilt and pain. It simply didn't make any sense to go on.

Catherine recalled the dark night many years ago when she had tried to end her life in a similar fashion. She remembered waking in a hospital room. She had been saved from the abyss of death by a neighbor who claimed she saw Catherine take the sleeping pills in a dream and rescued her in time. She told Catherine this story when she visited Catherine in the hospital.

Catherine had said hello a few times when the neighbor waved and returned the hello. The neighbor came over one time offering friendship. She asked some questions but Catherine was reticent about her past and gave brief answers. Catherine sent strong signals that she just wanted to be left alone.

During her recovery, Catherine endured extensive psychiatric examinations and began on a path towards a normal life with the aid of significant therapy and medication. When Catherine came home from the mental hospital she refused to accept any further contact from the neighbor who had intervened and stopped Catherine's plans to end her miserable life. Catherine immediately found a new place to live. The neighbor's concern for Catherine's wellbeing had frightened her. Catherine was determined to live a carefully cloistered life. She would have no contact with her new neighbors.

"I wonder how that lady is now," Catherine thought to herself, "no one will be able to rescue me now. They don't even know where I live." Even her doctor was unaware of her actual address as she used a post office box for all of her correspondence and never notified him of her relocation. Soon, Catherine slipped into an unconscious state. She had left the nightstand lamp on.

Carol drove slowly over the slippery roads hoping to prevent hitting a patch of black ice. The night was very cold but the stars were bright. She finally found Sycamore and pulled onto the street. It was dark road with few streetlights. Even in the blackness of the night, the street seemed very familiar to Carol and her heart then began to pound. The further she drove up the street the more convinced she became that this was indeed the street she had seen in her dream.

Carol couldn't recognize the house numbers in the dark so she decided to park her car and trudge through the snow and ice. It was a treacherous walk, completely unlike the pleasant stroll in her dream. She finally found the house numbered 944. It was completely dark. She gently knocked on the door. Carol rubbed her nippy fingers together and wished she had put on warmer gloves. She knocked louder but got no response. She peered through the window in front and then detected a dim light towards the back of the house.

Carol took a deep breath and then turned towards the back of the house where the light was. She had to go through the gate, which proved very difficult with the lingering snowdrifts.

"I must be crazy to be doing this. I hope nobody calls the police on me," Carol mumbled in the dark. Still, she felt urgent to see who was in the house any way she could. She approached the back of the house and spotted the window with dim light shining through. Fortunately, the window had curtains with a few tiny gaps for peering through.

A feeling of eerie Déjà vu swept over Carol as she carefully glanced through the curtains into the very dimly lit room. She saw a woman asleep in the bed and beside her, an empty pill bottle. After a minute of careful gazing, she recognized the face to be that of Catherine. Carol gasped at the sight once again and put her hand to her mouth and exclaimed, "I can't believe this!" She grabbed her purse and looked through it to find her cell phone. It was so hard to find in the dark with her cold shaky hands. She called 911, told the dispatcher what she suspected and planned to wait in her car for the ambulance to arrive. She glanced through the curtains once more before leaving to her car. Looking around the room, something interesting caught Carol's attention in the corner. It looked like a Christmas decoration in the shape of a house with some lights on it.

# *December 11ᵗʰ*

Catherine's eyes opened slowly and she glanced around the room. She could hear the noise of a busy emergency room around her but all she saw was tall grayish curtains surrounding her medical bed. She became aware of the IV line in her arm. Her stomach and throat hurt, and she felt dizzy. Catherine closed her eyes in anguish at the reality of being back in a hospital emergency room. She did not want to be here. How was it possible that once again she wasn't successful at ending her miserable existence? Who had found her this time? Catherine felt angry. She did not want to continue. The doctors had pumped her stomach of the medication. She felt terrible, both emotionally and physically. When she attempted her first suicide, she still had some resolve to make a second go at her life but now, she just felt flat. There was no desire left.

She felt so depressed about her work and how her boss had treated her. Catherine was sure there was no hope of ever returning to where her emotions were under control so she could live behind that composed stoic mask she had worn for so long. As long as that imaginary wooden house with the little lit up windows continued to haunt her about her past, she would be an emotional wreck. She couldn't hold her emotions in anymore. The dam was broken.

The problem with the advent calendar house was the fact that it wasn't imaginary, not in the true sense of the word, at least to Catherine. It had the ability to invade her mind. She could touch and feel it. It looked as real to her as anything she'd ever seen in her life. It was not a plain piece of wood. It was extraordinarily beautiful. It was magical. It could mysteriously appear and disappear without any logical explanation. No, it was real in some unexplainable supernatural way. She realized that because it was real to her and no one else, she would never be able to return back to her normal life. She could never be considered sane again since no one else could see it. It had somehow transferred her from a dreary safe life into her own personal episode of The Twilight Zone. Catherine wondered what memory it would conjure up today. At least she wouldn't have to see it today. It would have to stay at her house while she remained in the hospital. Or maybe, somehow, it would show up again by her bedside or the latest view would play in her inside her mind. At this point, Catherine almost laughed at the thought. Any humor in the situation however, was overshadowed by the realization of having yet another prison stay at the hospital while the doctors did their best to analyze and medicate her.

Catherine lay quietly in bed feeling deeply anguished. As much as she wanted to die to end her suffering, it was obvious to Catherine now that she couldn't end her life. It was as if some unseen power had intervened again to prevent her suicide. Before long Dr. Thomas entered the room. Catherine turned her head away from him and sighed deeply. He didn't respond but stood there looking at his deeply troubled patient. Finally he talked to Catherine.

"I'm terribly sorry to find you here in this hospital bed this afternoon, Catherine, but I am so grateful you were found in time. I tried to find you yesterday but the address I have in my records is obviously incorrect. You never contacted me once. I thought we agreed that you would contact me when you felt any change in your condition."

Catherine shut her eyes tightly and didn't respond. Her eyes became moistened with tears. She wished he would just disappear or that she could just vanish. She didn't want to talk. She didn't want to be in this terrible boat again. She was tired of medication. She didn't want to take any more of it. She remembered showing the calendar house to Dr. Thomas and he just saw a piece of wood and that was all. He couldn't help her, which was obvious. However, she was his prisoner, at least for now. How could she ever convince him now that she was okay after she tried suicide again? Catherine was not well. She thought she could never be well again. Perhaps Dr. Thomas would commit her to a mental institution and she would never leave. Catherine felt as if she had just entered her own personal hell.

Dr. Thomas scribbled notes on the chart and decided to leave. He would return later. Catherine had never ignored him before. She had obviously descended to a new low. He would have to discuss with others doctors to determine a new protocol to follow with her, as she had suddenly become one of his most challenging patients. Dr. Thomas looked sadly at the miserable patient curled up under the white hospital blankets with her back turned to him. He was amazed at how quickly she had declined and shook his head in disbelief as he left her bedside.

Catherine decided to ignore all medical personnel that came into the room that day. She made a terrible patient. She didn't care. She was angry at the fact she was still alive. Later that day, arrangements were being made for her to return to the West Valley Mental Hospital for an extended stay. Catherine said nothing as the emergency room doctor explained the arrangements ordered by Dr. Thomas.

Carol Jones had thought a lot about Catherine all day. Last night she had driven over to the emergency room to see how Catherine was doing but was told nothing about her condition. She wanted to talk to Catherine but at the same time, she felt very nervous about trying to make contact with a woman that really didn't want anything to do with her. The problem was that Carol just couldn't seem to get Catherine off her mind. Carol worked at a downtown retail store and being just fourteen days before Christmas, the clothing store was busier than normal.

Carol was a little older than Catherine. She had a pleasant looking face with some deep set wrinkles around her eyes and mouth, indicators of her difficult life as a single mother. Her light brown hair had streaks of gray. She had deep blue eyes that seem to twinkle every now and then and a smile that was contagious. She had one daughter, Megan, who lived about four hours away. Carol enjoyed any time she could to visit her daughter and see her little two year-old grandson named Seth. Carol had been single for many years after her first husband abandoned Carol right after she gave birth to their infant daughter. Carol struggled to raise her daughter as a single mother. At times her life left her feeling bitter. Agonizing loneliness and persistent poverty almost did her in from time to time but it was the love for Megan, and support from her mother, which got her through the toughest days. Carol felt grateful for her little family.

Thankfully, her heart healed enough to let a friendly man who seemed to visit the retail store quite often, a chance to take her to dinner and a movie one night. She and John Jones developed a wonderful friendship over time. He was very patient with Carol but finally insisted on marriage when his feelings for her grew way beyond friendship. Her daughter was a teenager by this point and provided some resistance to the match. John persisted, Carol finally conceded and the marriage proved to be a happy one. Carol had learned to trust her heart to someone again.

It was time for her lunch break and Carol decided to try the hospital one more time. She quickly drove over to the emergency room to inquire about Catherine. The nurse tried to brush her off but Carol felt the strength to persist. Her pleading and admitting to the fact that she was the person who found Catherine unconscious convinced the nurse to try to get some information about her condition. After holding on the phone for a long time, the nurse was finally informed that arrangements had been made for Catherine to be transferred to West Valley Mental Health Hospital. The nurse receptionist informed Carol that Catherine was under the care of Dr. Wayne Thomas. Carol expressed her gratitude, left the hospital, gobbled down a sandwich at the deli and returned immediately to work.

Catherine continued her silent treatment to all who had the unfortunate responsibility to interact with her in the hospital that day. She was sure if she opened her mouth, the anger would gush out, so she chose to pen it up, for now. She was done with the routine of mental wards but here she was again on her way to another one. Catherine felt incredible resentment towards her unknown rescuer.

After she was checked into her hospital room, Dr. Thomas came in for another visit, but he could tell immediately that Catherine's demeanor hadn't softened much. She just stared at him blankly when he asked how she was doing. He waited patiently for a response but gave up after a few minutes deciding he needed a different approach to begin recovery therapy with Catherine. He returned to his office and found a note to call a lady named Carol Jones. Having never heard of this woman, he cast aside the note and went to discuss Catherine's case with a colleague.

Later that night, Carol Jones struggled to get to sleep. Normally she slept fairly well, but the events of the past two days seemed to occupy her mind and she felt frustrated at the level of concern she felt for Catherine. She wanted to talk to Catherine but her fear stopped her. She hoped the doctor would be available in the morning so she could at least talk to him about the situation she found herself in. Carol wanted to just forget the whole thing ever happened but in some mysterious way, she had a connection to this mentally and emotionally troubled woman.

Finally her anxiety lessened and she fell asleep. Carol's dream that night was the most amazing dream she ever had in her life. It was a very realistic dream, even more than the one she had the previous night. She really felt like she was physically there. Carol was taking a journey, a long walk in a thick mist. She had the sense of walking for a long time and feeling much despair at being lost with no idea where she was going when she came upon a house. The house was large and it had many windows, some of which were lit. She peered inside the first window and saw a girl's bedroom with a bed covered with a pink bedspread and some toys on a shelf. Next to the bed was a small table set up with a tiny china tea set. Seated at the tiny table was a little girl playing with her doll. Carol admired the happy little scene but then her attention was diverted to a little redheaded boy who ran past her into the mist.

Carol turned back to the house and desired to peer into more of the lit windows out of curiosity when she realized each window had a number on it painted in gold. She gazed up at the interesting looking house and counted twenty-four numbered windows. Most of the windows were too high up for her to see into. Carol noticed there was one more lit window she could easily see into with the number 11 on it. She looked in the window and saw a small Christmas tree decorated with a little strand of colored lights and a few simple ornaments. Seated next to the tree were a little baby girl and her parents, watching joyfully as their daughter tried to unwrap a small Christmas gift.  They were helping her tear off the colorful paper.  It was a precious scene to behold. Suddenly Carol awoke from her vivid ream and gasped in the darkness.

# *December 12ᵗʰ*

Carol had trouble sleeping again after her troubling dream. She pondered on what it could mean on and off during the night. Finally, when she could stand the sleeplessness no more, she got up and went to the living room to watch a movie, hoping to drive any thoughts of the dream out of her mind for a time. It seemed to work as she found a murder mystery on her favorite cable television station. Carol loved to solve mysteries. She read every mystery novel she could find. Her own mystery dream was another story, however, as she wished it gone from her mind. She dozed off after a while on the couch and was awakened by her husband as he got up for his morning work shift at a local factory.

"What are you doing on the couch?" John asked as he tied his shoes. Carol sat up and stared at him for a moment.

"I couldn't sleep. I had another dream last night. It was so vivid. I don't know what's wrong with me? All of a sudden I am having these strange dreams. I haven't had any dreams for quite some time and now they seems to be happening all the time. The dream I had about Catherine's house and then going over to her house and finding Catherine unconscious again? Phew, it's really weird."

John nodded his head in agreement. After a minute of silence between the two, he asked, "What dream did you have last night?"

"It was like I was really there in my dream. I could feel the cool mist on my face as I was walking through it. I had no idea where I was going and I started to panic. It seemed like hours I was walking along this path that seemed to go nowhere in particular at all except straight forward. Suddenly I came upon this big house. It was just full of windows. I remember counting 24 windows!"

"That's really strange," John added.

"That's not even the strangest thing. Some of the windows were lit up and I could see people inside. I saw this couple sitting next to a Christmas tree with a little baby and then I suddenly woke up. That's all I remember except for some little redheaded kid running past me. I don't know what to think about it," Carol admitted, rubbing her forehead in exhaustion.

"Wasn't your other dream about a house too? Maybe there is a connection," John suggested.

Carol shrugged her shoulders and thought for a moment. Her eyes got wide with excitement when she realized the lady in the window with the baby girl did resemble Catherine somewhat, although it was kind of a stretch. Maybe it really was Catherine, Carol thought excitedly.

"You know, I think there might be one. The lady in the window kind of looked like a very young version of Catherine. If that's the case, boy, she's really aged. That house reminds me of something too I saw at Catherine's room when I went over there the other night although I couldn't see it very well. I thought it was some kind of weird Christmas decoration or something," Carol responded as she got up from the couch to go fix some breakfast.

"I really need to talk to her doctor today," Carol declared as she fixed her husband his breakfast of oatmeal, toast and coffee,"I wonder why he didn't return my call yesterday."

"What are you going to talk to him about? Does he even know that you found her again?"

"I don't think so. The only way I found out anything about Catherine was from the nurse at the emergency room. After a tremendous amount of sincere pleading, she finally told me the doctor's name. I just feel like I need to talk to him about what's been happening to me. Maybe he can tell Catherine about my dreams. I don't think she ever wants to see me again," Carol responded as she looked around her darkened living room, "You know, John, we need to think about getting a Christmas tree put up, don't you think? It's getting awfully close to Christmas. I haven't even started doing any shopping except for what I have in lay-away at work. There is always so much to do at Christmas that I don't have time for!" Carol added. John just shrugged his shoulders at the thought of getting a tree already. John didn't care too much about celebrating Christmas. He liked to keep things simple. Setting up a tree on Christmas Eve was more his style.

Carol looked at the time and groaned. It was too early for her to get up yet. Normally, John fixed breakfast before heading off to work. This morning he appreciated Carol making his breakfast. He kissed her on the forehead and thanked her quietly for the favor before he left. Carol sat staring at the wall while she collected her thoughts before pausing again to think about the strange dream haunting her during the night. She kept thinking about seeing a happy and youthful looking Catherine in the window with her young family trying to imagine what must have happened to them and why she was now such a lonely miserable person. Carol's heart yearned for understanding and the desire to help Catherine in any way she could. She decided to take a relaxing bath to help sooth her thoughts and prepare for another busy day at the store. She still had some shopping to do to find the desired gifts for her daughter and grandson.

The night had been difficult for Catherine. Her emotions were still a mix of extreme anger and frustration. She didn't sleep well until a nurse noticed her sleeplessness and brought her some sleep medication. It helped some but her nerves seemed to resist any major calming down. Now she stared at the drab colored wall of her hospital room and wished for escape from the dreary prison. She wondered about the calendar house and what new scene would be displaying in it today. Part of her longed to see it again but the resentment she felt towards this emotionally tormenting object completely dominated her mind.

She heard some whistling coming down the hall and all at once the figure of a large black man appeared in her doorway. It was Maurice who was bringing her breakfast.

"Well, if it isn't Miss Catherine. You've returned I see."

Catherine didn't respond. She turned her head towards the wall at his comment.

"Well I am glad to see you here. Remember that each day we have to live is a wonderful precious gift. You enjoy it, now, you hear? Here's some delicious food to help you appreciate the food that's waiting for you when get back to the real world again," Maurice remarked with a happy chuckle. Catherine looked over at the unappealing bowl of oatmeal on the tray with two slices of buttered toast and shook her head in disgust. She glared at him but he just flashed a big warm smile that seemed to help melt some of her anger. She quickly turned away from him again and didn't respond when he said goodbye and began to whistle another Christmas tune, "I'm dreaming of a White Christmas" as he left.

After a few minutes, Dr. Thomas once again appeared in her room to attempt a more successful interview with his disturbed patient.

"Hello, Catherine. I hope that you were able to get some rest last night," Dr. Thomas said in his most pleasant tone of voice, hoping to get a favorable response from Catherine. She looked up at the doctor and shook her head in disgust and turned away from him.

"Go away!" Catherine thought to herself. She still refused to speak to the doctor. She was embarrassed to be in this boat again with him. She felt it was as if she had made absolutely no progress with him after all this time. She was back to square one and she simply didn't want to go forward again. She just looked away as tears stung her tired eyes. The silence became unbearable to the doctor. He just couldn't understand how their relationship had taken such a reversal to the point where she wouldn't even speak to him anymore. Part of him wanted to transfer her case to another doctor out of pure frustration but his desire to help her out of this latest episode of emotional depression was stronger than ever. He couldn't believe that she would try to kill herself over a piece of wood. It was almost beyond belief and in all of his cases to date, by far the most bizarre for him to fathom.

Dr. Thomas decided to read out loud to Catherine his notes about the last week of her recent episode to possibly trigger some kind of response from her. Perhaps then he might be able to make some kind of inroad to begin therapy with her again.

"Catherine Daley, patient, came to my office today, December 3rd to discuss some recent experience she's had with an object found at her door on the evening of December 1st. She stated the object is a wooden house that shows her images from her past in little windows. She also believes that her deceased daughter brought the object to her door as she saw this happen in a dream the night after she received the object at her door. I checked her prescription for Thorazine and increased her dosage by 30 percent. We discussed a previous delusional episode. Patient left office not convinced it was a delusion and wanted to bring the object in for me to review. I conceded to allow her to bring it in the next day."

"December 4th, Catherine Daley, patient, came to my office with object discussed about on previous day. I found it to be nothing more than a piece of wood, roughly resembling the shape of a house but nothing like patient described seeing. I filled out paperwork for patient to be admitted to West Valley Mental

Hospital to receive required treatment for new delusional episode. Patient committed to stay at hospital."

Dr. Thomas paused, and then looked up hopefully from his report at Catherine to see any change in her behavior. She continued to look away and showed no change in her behavior, so he continued to read. Catherine pretended not to listen but was aggravated every time Dr. Thomas referred to her as "patient". It seemed so typical of him to be so uncompassionate about such things. She wanted to scream at him while he continued his monologue on the day to day unraveling of his pathetic patient. It was particularly difficult for Catherine to be reminded of her behavior at the hospital when staff attempted to remove the wooden object from her possession and when she reacted violently after imagining the calendar house in her mind and had to be subdued. It sounded even worse when Dr. Thomas read his dreary summary of the events that had taken place in the last twelve days. Dr. Thomas had no comments on any possible reasons for all of this except to say now and then that his patient was suffering from the effects of extreme loneliness, which was a major contributing factor for her mental and emotional decline.

Dr. Thomas was almost finished with reading his report when the nurse came into the room to tell him that he had an important phone call waiting in his office. He looked at Catherine for a moment, and rubbed his forehead out of frustration. She still hadn't budged from her position and he could not tell if anything he had read had even been heard. He sighed heavily and then left the room. He was relieved to have a break from his frustrating patient. He walked down the hall to his office at the hospital.

"Hello, this is Dr. Thomas."

"Yes, Dr. Thomas? Hi, my name is Carol Jones. I really need to talk to you about your patient, Catherine Daley," pleaded Carol nervously on the phone.

"What is this in regards to?" Dr. Thomas inquired.

"Well, I was the one who found her unconscious and called the ambulance," Carol answered. There was a long pause.

"Are you her neighbor or something?" Dr. Thomas asked.

"Not any more. I used to be. I was the one who found her last time when she tried to overdose. Is she going to be all right?"

"Let me get this straight," Dr. Thomas interrupted. "You found her unconscious both times?"

"Yes, sir," Carol answered quietly.

"If you are not her neighbor now, how did you know she was unconscious? Did you try to call or something?"

"No. I didn't have her phone number or even her current address. It's kind of strange how I found out," Carol hesitated to go on.

"So, how did you find out?" Dr. Thomas probed.

"I had a very realistic dream on the night she took the pills. I dreamt I was walking on a street that was named Sycamore and stopped in front of a certain house. I even saw the number on the house. Then I woke up. I wrote down the number of the house. It was all very strange. I had never seen that house before in my life. Then it occurred to me it might be Catherine's house and that she might be in trouble again. I only thought that because my husband said a man looking like a doctor came by earlier in the evening asking about a lady who used to live in the place across the street. We decided he must have been trying to find out about Catherine. She used to live there. I ventured out in the night, drove over to a Sycamore street I saw on a map in the phonebook, and there was the house. I looked around the house and discovered Catherine in her bedroom because the curtains were slightly parted. I then called the ambulance," Carol answered.

"You know, I was that man your husband talked to. I went looking for her the other night because I was very worried since I hadn't heard from her for some time and I couldn't reach her by phone. I went and looked at what I thought was her residence. I asked your husband about her but he didn't know anything. I was trying to find her at home but the place looked empty. She had moved and never updated me on her current address. All her medical mail was sent to a post office box," Dr. Thomas added excitedly, "So you had a dream that showed you where she lived? That is amazing!"

"Yes, it is. Dr. Thomas, I'd like to share a few more things I have recently experienced that might be related to Catherine. Can I come and talk to you, and possibly even see Catherine?" Carol asked meekly.

"Of course you can. I am very interested in finding out more about what has happened. Yes, please come to my office. Do you have time today?" Dr. Thomas inquired anxiously.

"I can come during my lunch today. It's pretty busy at the store where I work at because it is getting so close to Christmas so I won't be able to stay long," Carol responded. She got directions to the hospital from the doctor, hung up the phone and then returned to work. Dr. Thomas sat in utter amazement pondering on the conversation he just had. He felt hopeful about Catherine. He decided to leave her alone for the rest of the morning.

Dr. Thomas was excited about meeting Carol. She informed him of her history with Catherine and how intervening on Catherine's behalf the first time had caused Catherine to shun any attempts at friendship. Carol told Dr. Thomas how she felt a connection to Catherine despite what had happened. Dr. Thomas asked in detail about her dream and the events that led her to find Catherine once again unconscious from an overdose.

"You seem to be Catherine's guardian angel," Dr. Thomas commented after Carol finished telling him her story of finding Catherine, "how did you know to call me?"

"I pleaded with the nurse at the emergency room and explained a bit about how I had found her and that I needed to talk to her doctor more about it. Thankfully, she gave me your name," Carol answered.

"I had another really vivid dream last night and I think it was about Catherine too."

"Oh really? What was it about?" Dr. Thomas asked.

"This dream was even more realistic than the previous night. I was walking again; it seemed, for a long time in a mist. I felt very afraid I was lost and then suddenly I came across this big house. It had a lot of windows. Twenty four to be exact," Carol answered.

"Did you say a house with twenty four windows?" Dr. Thomas interrupted.

"Yes. Some of them were lit up. I looked into a couple of them. I saw a little girl playing at a table with a doll in one of them, and in the other one, there was a couple sitting by a Christmas tree watching their baby try to open a Christmas present. It was a very precious scene." Upon hearing this, Dr. Thomas's eyes opened very wide and he dropped the pencil he was taking notes with.

"You know, the woman in the scene looked very much like a young Catherine. It is very strange. And, oh yes, there were numbers on each of the windows, painted in gold. That's all I can remember and then I woke up. I couldn't go back to sleep the rest of the night," Carol added.

Dr. Thomas sat shocked in his chair, not sure what to say next. It seemed that this woman had a dream that matched Catherine's imagined calendar house. What could this all mean? It boggled his mind and he could not fathom the meaning.

"Dr. Thomas, what do you think of this dream? Could it be related to Catherine?" Carol asked. Dr. Thomas stared at Carol for a moment and then spoke, "I think it does."

Dr. Thomas decided it was time to talk to Catherine. He led Carol down the hall to Catherine's room. She was in bed, trying to read a book when they came in.

"Catherine, I have Carol Jones with me. She was the one who found you unconscious in your room and called the ambulance," Dr. Thomas announced.

Catherine looked up and glared at both of them. She said nothing.

"Catherine, Carol has informed me that she had a dream the other night and it seems to have included something you are very familiar with. She described to me a house with twenty-four windows and she saw scenes inside two of these windows, one of which matched what you described to me when you first brought in the calendar house. She described seeing a little girl playing at a table with a doll."

Catherine's eyes became wide and she covered her dropped open mouth with her hand.

"Catherine, I think it would be in your best interest to talk to Carol about what she saw. I will leave you two alone for a few minutes, "Dr. Thomas said as he looked at a nervous Carol, and gently nodded his head to reassure her.

The silence was awkward for a few minutes. Catherine was still in shock. Carol decided to break the ice and ask about her past.

"Catherine, were you married once?"

Catherine broke her silence by answering yes. Carol asked if she had a little girl and Catherine told her about her three children and husband who were now deceased. Carol's heart ached as Catherine shared her sad misfortune. Carol decided to focus on the dream about the house.

"Catherine, in the dream I had, I saw what looked like you and your husband with your first daughter next to a Christmas tree. Your daughter was trying to open a Christmas present. It was a most precious scene to behold."

Catherine eyes filled with tears as Carol described what she saw in the window. Catherine's mind immediately went back to the memory of little Susie opening her first Christmas present. It was one of those precious scenes stored away by the mind but easily recalled when triggered.

"What number was on the window?" Catherine asked.

"I think it was eleven," Carol answered. Catherine smiled as she thought about the calendar house, wishing she could see the scene herself. Suddenly, Catherine realized what this all possibly meant. If Carol saw the scene in her dream, perhaps she could see it in real life as well.

"Did Dr. Thomas tell you about my calendar house?" Catherine asked. Carol shook her head.

"I have this wooden house that shows me exactly what you saw in your dream. Nobody else can see it but me," Catherine declared, "it has reminded me of my past and what I have lost. My heart can't take it any longer. Everyone thinks I'm completely crazy. I just got tired of fighting any longer so I took the pills. You found me unconscious, again, and here I am," Catherine added flatly.

"Where did you get this wooden house?" Carol asked excitedly.

"It was on my doorstep when I came home from work about twelve days ago. It was wrapped in this very interesting looking paper and had no address or anything written on it. I was quite surprised to find it there, I felt frightened by it and I didn't open it until I had a dream about it that night. I saw in my dream my youngest daughter Jenny put it on my doorstep."

"You're kidding!" Carol exclaimed.

"No, I really saw my daughter in my dream and it seemed so real to me," Catherine responded. The hairs on Carol's arms seemed to stand on end when Catherine mentioned having a realistic dream.

"So this house came from somewhere else? Maybe it came from heaven, perhaps? That's really weird but pretty cool too!" Carol thought out loud.

"I used to believe in all that stuff about heaven and God. I can't say for sure now but it seems like it is one of the only ways to explain the house's existence. I really don't know what to think about it. I am hopeful that I haven't really lost my mind because you seem to share in this experience by having a dream about it," Catherine added. She turned and looked down for a few minutes and then looked up at Carol.

"I have the wooden house at my house right now. Dr. Thomas had taken it away from me but it showed up again at my door. I would love for you to see it," Catherine urged. Carol thought for a moment about the other night when she looked in Catherine's room and saw an interesting looking object on the floor that reminded her of a Christmas decoration lit up.

"Was it in your bedroom?" Carol asked excitedly. Catherine nodded.

"I think I saw it! I saw something that reminded me of a house that was partly lit up. I thought it was a Christmas decoration of some kind."

"Could you go to my house? I want to see it again so bad. Could you get it for me?" Catherine asked.

"Of course. Is your house locked?" Carol answered. Catherine looked in her purse.

"I don't know, but here are my keys just in case. Call me when you get there and let me know. Here is the phone number to call me here."

Catherine wrote down the number and handed it to Carol. Carol stood up and just as she was leaving, Dr. Thomas came back in the room. He could tell immediately that things had changed dramatically for Catherine. Carol excused herself and said goodbye and informed Catherine she wouldn't be able to check until after work. She left the hospital as quickly as she could. Dr. Thomas pulled up a chair and began to once again converse with his patient and help her on the road to recovery.

Carol returned to work completely excited about the turn of events. Fortunately the afternoon went by quickly because of the steady flow of holiday shoppers. She was so relieved to get off work and she headed straight over to Catherine's house. Once inside Catherine's bedroom, she saw the calendar house next to Catherine's bed. Carol picked it up and gasped as she examined it. It was incredibly beautiful, unlike anything she had ever beheld in her life. She carefully looked at each lit up window, her heart pounding as she realized she was looking at scenes from Catherine's precious past. She noticed that the window with the number one painted on it had the same scene as she saw in her dream except there was no little girl in it. It was just the room with the doll, miniature tea set and table. In window eleven, there was the little Christmas gift partially unwrapped sitting next to the simply decorated Christmas tree but the little family was absent in the scene.

Carol now looked at the lit up window with a twelve painted on it. It was a living room, decorated brightly with lovely Christmas decorations, a beautiful tree with shining with lights, tinsel and many colorful ornaments surrounded by all shapes and sizes of Christmas gifts, and a large fireplace with a mantle. Hanging down from the mantle were five Christmas stockings filled to the brim with all the little gifts and goodies of the season. It was so warm and inviting. The loving home looked so charming. Carol wished she could have had such a Christmas scene in her home.

She looked around for a phone and found one in the kitchen and proceeded to call Catherine at the hospital.

"Hello?" Catherine answered.

"Hi Catherine. This is Carol Jones. I am at your home. I just found the wooden house in your bedroom. It's breathtaking! You never mentioned how stunning it was. The scenes are amazing. The one for the twelfth is the most beautiful of all."

"What! What? You see the scenes? You really do? What is the twelfth window about?" Catherine asked excitedly.

Carol proceeded to describe the incredibly quaint Christmas scene in detail. Catherine knew at once what it was from. Carol described the living room scene from the last joyous Christmas Eve the Daley family had spent together. Tears streamed from Catherine's eyes as she thanked Carol tenderly, asked her to take the calendar house home, bring it to the hospital the next day and then she hung up the phone.

# December 13ᵗʰ

It was a brand new day for Catherine. She woke up and felt more hopeful than she had in years. Despite the events of the past two weeks, even with giving into the ultimate feelings of despair and attempting to end her precious life only two days previous, Catherine felt different. She welcomed the day. She didn't know what it would bring but she felt no longer alone in the world. There was a person now who Catherine felt a connection to. The world can seem incredibly cold and lonely until a person builds bridges of friendship to others. Only then can burdens be lightened, fears eased, hearts warmed and precious memories made.

During her sessions with Dr. Thomas the previous afternoon, she revealed very little to him about what happened between her and Carol. She felt Dr. Thomas was helpful to some extent but he couldn't share in the miracle that had happened to both women. He couldn't see the calendar house for himself. He saw only wood. Still, Dr. Thomas seemed to be more understanding than he had previously been. He did admit to Catherine that Carol Jones had surprised him with her seeing things in her dreams that sounded so similar to Catherine's. He had absolutely no logical explanation for all of this and didn't know what to write down in his medical notes about the case. Dr. Thomas chose instead to focus on the existence of severe depression and despondency that led to Catherine's second suicide attempt. She obviously still had major chemical brain imbalances that needed additional medical treatment and more effective coping skills to help her manage the day to day challenges of her life. He was grateful just to resume conversations with Catherine after the silent treatment she had given him.

Carol showed the calendar house to her husband when she first got home from Catherine's house and for various reasons, he saw nothing but wood as well.

"Isn't this beautiful?" Carol declared excitedly to John when she found him sitting on the couch watching a television show.

"What?" John asked as he looked at Carol. "What are you talking about?"

"This house! Isn't it incredible looking?"

John grabbed the calendar house from Carol and looked at it, and handed it back to her.

"It's a nice piece of wood but I wouldn't call it incredible or beautiful. Why are you calling it a house? It's just a piece of wood. Say, what's gotten into you honey, and why are you so late?"

Carol's mouth dropped open as she realized her husband was unable to see what she could so plainly see. Suddenly Carol felt very uncomfortable. Was she losing her mind too? Why couldn't John see the calendar house as well? What was going on here? She wasn't sure what to say next. She decided to laugh off his comment and told him that she was going to use the piece of wood for some craft project for Christmas. John shrugged his shoulders and returned his attention back to the television program. She went to the kitchen to fix dinner and put the beautifully carved wooden house carefully down on the dining table. Her mind went over the events of the past few days. Everything seemed quite remarkable and very real to her. The dreams had been alarmingly realistic. She definitely didn't feel like the whole thing with the calendar house had been in her imagination. Then she thought about Catherine. Catherine had been dealing with these feelings for almost two weeks wondering why on earth this calendar house was only visible to her. Catherine had questioned her own sanity and now Carol was questioning hers.

She sat down at the table and once again studied the amazing wooden house up close. It shimmered in the kitchen light as she turned it from front to back. The wood was rich in brown hues but it also had a unique iridescent glow about it that reminded one of heavenly light. Carol enjoyed viewing the little lit up windows showing the scenes of wonderful Christmas memories. She especially loved the scene of the small town gazebo decorated for the season and the vision of a simple but beautiful Christmas wedding. As she carefully examined each little scene in detail, Carol wondered about each story surrounding the scenes and looked forward to Catherine sharing these stories with her. Suddenly John asking when dinner would be ready interrupted the delightful moment. He yelled that he was getting really hungry. She put down the house and got up to make a hamburger and noodle casserole. She put the calendar house in a bag by the front door so she would remember to take it the next day.

Carol had a fitful night of sleep and was grateful that it was now day and time to get up. Her worries about being sane had overshadowed her subconscious and she had shadowy dreams about mental institutions and being committed to one forever. It was very disturbing to Carol. She preferred a night's sleep with no dreams at all. She hurried around trying to get a few decorations put up that she had taken out of a box the previous night before she went to bed. Her husband had mentioned the piece of wood again before going to sleep and wondered what she was going to do with that. Carol told him that she didn't know yet. She enjoyed the quiet of the morning before work with her husband gone as she could do a few things she never seemed to get done in the evenings.

She grabbed the bag with the calendar house inside and peaked into it. Carol noticed that a new miniature window was lit up with the number thirteen on it. She shook her head in astonishment at this incredible advent calendar. Normal advent calendars were little Christmas scenes or items hidden behind paper doors as part of a bigger Christmas scene to be opened each day before the twenty-fourth of Christmas but this advent calendar revealed the scenes each day by having them miraculously appear. She pulled out the house to carefully look at the newest lit up window. It didn't seem the same as the twelve previous windows. It didn't show anything obvious like before. It contained one item, a candle. From Carol's view of the window, the candle appeared to be floating in mid-air, which truly amazed her. It was a deep color of red and had a green wreath decorated with glitter on the side. Carol thought it was very pretty but wondered why the window didn't reveal a scene of Christmas like the rest of the windows had. She looked forward to bringing the calendar house to Catherine later during her lunch break.

Catherine sat in bed, anxious to see Carol again. It had been years since she felt such a desire to visit with another woman. Dr. Thomas was making his best efforts at re-establishing a good doctor/patient relationship with Catherine and she was cooperative. She longed to be outside the walls of her hospital room. She thought about her job and wondered if she would go back to it after what had transpired there just a few days earlier. She felt very uncomfortable about her boss now. She did not trust him and doubted she could ever do so again. Catherine got dressed and began to wander down the hall in search of something to satisfy her frustration and restlessness. She ended up in the therapy room again ready to sit and do a puzzle to get her mind off things for a while until Carol showed up again.

Dr. Thomas appeared in the room about an hour later. He smiled when he saw Catherine up and dressed and not pining away in her room. He sat down at the table next to her.

"How are you feeling today, Catherine?" He asked in a pleasant voice. Catherine looked at him and smiled and nodded her head. "You're doing well at putting that puzzle together I see."

"I'd like to leave, Dr. Thomas. I am feeling restless here."

"That's understandable, but I don't think you are quite ready to leave yet. I have to make sure this time that your mind is quite stable and that you can handle your emotions better without resorting to suicide again. We almost lost you, my dear."

"Don't I seem much better to you now? It's like the storm has passed and the sun is shining again in my life," Catherine responded hopefully.

"Well, you do not seem to be so melancholy as before but I am not convinced that the storm is completely over. Seems like you said this all before just a few days ago and looked at what happened."

"I know, but that was before."

"Before what?" Dr. Thomas asked.

"Carol."

"You still haven't told me much concerning the conversation you had with Carol. That might help me in my diagnosis of your condition and a prognosis of your progress and getting released from here."

Catherine hesitated before she spoke. "Well, Dr. Thomas, Carol really did help me to feel saner about everything that has happened to me since the first of the month. I almost feel happy about what's happened. I just can't explain any of it, that's what is troubling me still."

Dr. Thomas questioned Catherine more intently about the conversation with Carol but she didn't care to divulge anything except the conversation had to do with the dreams about the calendar house. When Catherine brought that up, Dr. Thomas simply said it was a coincidence that Carol had dreams similar to

Catherine's. Thankfully, the dreams were instructive to Carol to help her know that Catherine was in trouble again. However, he reminded Catherine that she needed to stop thinking about the piece of wood as anything but a piece of wood. Catherine felt like trying to object to his dismissal of the calendar house but decided it was probably for the best. If she continued to insist that there was any validity to it, she might never be able to leave the hospital. The calendar house would remain a secret between the ladies. Dr. Thomas left her alone again and she soon tired of the therapy room and went back to her room to read a dusty book she had grabbed that was sitting on a table.

As she walked down the hall to her room, she wondered and thought to herself, "What is this book? It looks familiar to me," She looked for the name of the book, dusted it off and found the name, *A Little Princess* by Frances Hodgson Burnett. "I know this book," said Catherine, "I read it when I was a little girl." She smiled and started to read the book. The book added to her growing happiness as she reminisced about the story first learned as a child. It was a magical experience to see the world through Sara Crewe's eyes and how well Sara endured the trials life brought her. Time passed quickly as she read the adored classic and eventually Carol showed up in her room.

"Catherine, how are you?" asked a smiling Carol as she walked in. "What are you reading?"

Catherine looked up and declared," Oh, Carol, it's so good to have you back! I'm reading a childhood classic, it's so wonderful," Catherine held up the book.

"A Little Princess? That's a great book. I loved reading it many years ago. It has a wonderful ending, doesn't it?"

"Yes. I love happy endings," Catherine added enthusiastically as she put the book down beside her, "Did you bring it?"

"Here it is," Carol showed the bag to Catherine.

"Quick, close the door!" urged Catherine, "I don't want to be interrupted by Dr. Thomas. He doesn't want to even discuss the calendar house. He only sees wood."

"That's just like my husband! I tried to show it to him last night and he only saw a piece of wood too. What is going on? Are we both crazy?" Carol added as she pulled the iridescent looking house from the bag and handed it to Catherine.

"Your husband didn't see it either? I guess it is just for you and me to see. I don't know why but the fact that you see it too means that both you and I are crazy or we're not crazy, just privileged. I am so thankful you see it too now. I am starting to feel really hopeful about my life ever since you called last night. The dark despondency I felt is being replaced with sweet hope."

Carol just smiled when she said that. Catherine looked delighted as she peered into each of the little newly lit windows.

She paused on the beautiful image shown in the twelfth window for a few minutes and tears formed in her eyes.

"This was the last Christmas eve that I spent with my children and husband. It was a wonderful occasion. The children had such a delightful time as we put on a little play about the first Christmas. Jenny dressed up her baby doll to be little Jesus and she played Mary. Even little Jimmy calmed down enough to be Joseph. My husband and I played the different parts of the shepherds and wise men and Susie was the angel. We played games, popped some corn and watched a Christmas movie. There was a sweet feeling of peace in our home that evening. You could really feel the children's joy in anticipation of Christmas morning. Oh how I miss those children! They were killed the following year just two days before Christmas," Catherine added sadly.

"Oh Catherine, I 'm so sorry. That twelfth window is such a bittersweet scene-so beautiful but so sad."

"I know. It was a great last Christmas together. You just never know when things like that are going to be your last. You just have to enjoy the moments as they come," Catherine sighed, wiping away some tears. She then glanced into the thirteenth window. She looked concerned when she saw the little red candle in it.

"That's strange. There is only a candle in this one. Where is the Christmas scene?" Catherine wondered.

"That's what I was marveling about. Something has changed but what does it mean?"

"I have no idea what it means or how it works. All I know is that it is here and that you and I both see it. That's the miracle! It must be real. It's so wonderful to see this again. Isn't it lovely?" Catherine noted joyfully as she lovingly caressed the smooth wood, "look at the way it's exquisitely painted." She moved it around to see how the light reflected off it in different positions like a person would do a shiny new penny.

"It's just beautiful," Carol added as she watched Catherine admire the unusual advent calendar that seemed to be turning both their lives upside down.

# *December 14ᵗʰ*

The ladies enjoyed their time together on the previous day. Carol had asked Catherine a few questions about the scenes in the windows. She was most curious about the Christmas gazebo and so she asked Catherine to share the story behind this scene. Carol was enraptured by the simple but precious love story of meeting James on the ice skating rink in the magical little town many Christmas seasons ago. Catherine once again felt a severe longing for her sweetheart James and was overcome by strong emotions. She openly wept. Carol reached out compassionately to Catherine for a hug. It had been years since another human being had hugged Catherine. The embrace brought much needed comfort and strength to her. Soon it was time for Carol to leave. Catherine asked Carol to go to her home and get some extra clothes for her which Carol was happy to do for Catherine. She promised to return the next day with the calendar and then said goodbye.

Both women tried to remain busy so the time would pass quickly until their next meeting. Carol found the store busier than ever when she returned so it was a snap to let the rush of holiday shoppers keep her mind occupied. She managed to get some shopping of her own done after work as her husband had taken on some overtime at the factory and would be home later than usual. Catherine, on the other hand, had an abundance of time on her hands. She had immensely enjoyed the classic novel and pondered on how wonderful books like that can be for the heart. She decided she wanted to find more books to read in the hospital and set off to search for another. Dr. Thomas had come to see her earlier in the afternoon for a therapy session and she participated to his satisfaction. He also was going to adjust her medication slightly. He felt hopeful that her mood seemed to be stabilizing and that any chemical imbalance in her brain was beginning to normalize. She had fallen asleep without sleep medication for the second night in a row and woke up feeling even more hopeful than the previous day.

Carol had checked the calendar house first thing when she woke up. The fourteenth window had what looked like a Yule log in it. That was even more puzzling to Carol than the candle had been. Hopefully it would make more sense to Catherine when she saw it later on in the day. Carol hurried and wrapped the gifts she had purchased the previous evening and headed off to work. The weather had turned colder and snow was in the forecast once again. It had been a snowy December so far and the prospects for a white Christmas seemed promising.

Dr. Thomas checked in on Catherine. She was engrossed in another novel and the therapy of reading good books seemed to be helping her overall wellbeing. Catherine was getting very tired of the hospital but most especially the food. She wanted to get some other food to eat and was scheming a way to get some. She decided to directly ask Dr. Thomas if she could get a pizza from her favorite Italian restaurant. He seemed amused by the idea but agreed to grant her wish later that day. Now Catherine had two things to look forward to.

By midafternoon Carol showed up with the calendar house hiding in her bag. She had also brought a submarine sandwich for two that she had picked up at a deli across the street from the store. Catherine was delighted to see the sandwich and genuinely thanked Carol for her thoughtfulness. Carol seemed so eager to be her friend and support. Catherine gratefully took the wooden calendar house from Carol.

"Wow, there is a Yule log in the window today. That's even stranger than yesterday. It seems like the windows will perhaps just show items from now on. You know, my dad's favorite Christmas tradition was getting a Yule log every year. Wait a minute, my mom always wanted to have a new Christmas candle," Catherine declared and then she covered her mouth in shock, "maybe these items have to do with my parents somehow."

"Really?" Carol asked.

"I wonder how they are doing," Catherine said quietly.

"Don't you talk to your parents?" Carol asked abruptly, quite shocked by Catherine's comment.

"No. I haven't talked to them for a very long time. I send them a Christmas card so they know I am still around."

Carol looked at Catherine with disbelief.

"You haven't talked to your parents in a very long time? Why not?"

"Oh, it's a long sad story."

Catherine proceeded to share with Carol a shortened version of the fight she had with her parents and how she had cut off ties with them after she was hurt and offended by their remarks following the breakdown. Catherine shook her head and fought back the tears. Carol sat quiet for a moment while she collected her thoughts.

"Don't you worry about how they are doing? How old are they? Have you heard from them at all?" Carol asked.

"I guess if they needed to reach me, they would. I just receive a card at Christmas from them as well but it never says anything but love, mom and dad. I just wish now I could go back in time to that horrible day and not get so mad and hurt by them. I'd like to see them again but I just can't."

"Well, you can't go back in time but there's no better time to do things like the present. The calendar house is here to help you Catherine. Maybe seeing those two items that reminded you of your parents is a cue that you need to fix your broken fences. You will never be happy until you do. You've already lost precious time with them. Call them!"

"I can't. They won't want to talk to me, I just know it."

"You don't know that. Do you know their number? I have my cell phone so you can call them right now if you want. You need to talk to them. Don't you feel that way?"

Catherine sat quietly thinking about what Carol had said. She looked at two of the little calendar house's windows, the ones which showed the knitted pink sweater and the bicycle, and she felt a pain in her heart that felt like a burning knife. She closed her eyes but the tears stung. Catherine's wet eyes further convinced Carol to persist in her encouragement.

"What can go wrong by calling them? Things probably couldn't get any worse between you and them. You can tell them you are sorry. Maybe they will forgive you and maybe they won't, but at least you will have made the first step and the pain and regret will diminish," reassured Carol encouragingly, "I don't know what I would do without my mom. She's been a lifesaver to me, especially during my darkest days after my husband abandoned me."

"I didn't know your husband abandoned you. I am so sorry to hear you had to go through that. It must have been terrible. What happened?"

"I guess he just didn't want to be a dad. We were young. You know the story. He couldn't handle it. I struggled as a single mom something terrible but my mother and God helped me get through it. Now my daughter is grown up, I have a great little grandson and a new husband who loves me."

"So, you believe in God?"

"Oh yes, I know there is someone up there that loves me and has helped get through each day. He will help you too. In fact, He's been helping you all along. He sent you this special gift," Carol picked up the house as she spoke.

"Despite all the pain I have had to go through, I suppose you're right." As Catherine spoke these words, her heart was filled with warmth and reassurance. She knew it was time to reach out and make the effort to try to reconnect with her parents.

Carol handed her the phone. It had been years since she had dialed the phone number for her parents but it came flooding back to her mind as she made the attempt. Catherine's hands shook as she held the phone. The phone rang a number of times and Catherine waited for the answering machine to pick up. She hesitated to speak but finally managed a brief message that said she was sorry and that she hoped they were doing well. She also mentioned being in the West Valley mental health hospital and they could reach her there. Then she then hung up and handed the phone back to Carol.

"Do you think they will call back?" Catherine asked Carol anxiously.

"I don't know. The ball is in their court now. They are probably going to be overjoyed at hearing from you and the communication not being in the form of some sterile Christmas card," Carol responded.

The women enjoyed eating the sandwich during the time remaining on Carol's lunch hour. Carol shared more of her past and some of the difficulties she faced and how she overcame many of the obstacles. Catherine felt inspired by her stories and encouraged by her strength. She was learning the value of friendship all over again but this time with a heart that was coming out of long cold winter. Carol shared more encouraging words about Catherine's attempt to reconnect with her parents before she left. Catherine felt hopeful that she had done the right thing and that things would get better somehow.  She would sit, read and wait for a promised pizza and a phone call that was years overdue.

# *December 15th*

The much anticipated phone call did come later the previous evening. Catherine sounded nervous as she spoke carefully to her mother. She thanked her for calling back.

"How's Dad doing?" Catherine managed to ask.

"He's been kind of sick lately I'm afraid to say," Catherine's mom answered, "he has cancer of the stomach."

Catherine gasped and she felt her heart drop at the news. "Oh Mom, I'm so sorry. How long has he had this?"

"We've known about six months."

"Why didn't you let me know?"

"I'm not sure. Anyhow, we've been busy seeking medical treatment. He's had about four chemotherapy treatments so far. He's resting right now from the one the other day. The prognosis so far looks promising."

Catherine's eyes welled up with tears. "Oh Mom, can you please forgive me for being so foolish all these years? I am so sorry dad is so sick."

"Well, we've been pretty foolish too for not trying harder to reach out to you. We just thought leaving you alone would be for the best. You were so miserable and unapproachable. So, why are you in a mental hospital again?"

Catherine hesitated before answering.

"Mom, I tried to commit suicide again."

There was a long pause and then a sigh.

"Oh dear. So you are not getting any better? I thought you had your depression somewhat under control with the doctor's help."

"I was doing pretty well for a long time, staying busy with work but something happened to me a couple of weeks ago that has upset my life pretty much. I was let go from my job and fell to pieces after that. I just lost all hope, that's all."

"What happened to make you lose your job?"

"I started to see things in this strange looking but beautiful object that I found on my door one evening. I was seeing things from my past like that pink sweater you knitted for me one Christmas."

"What?"

"I know it sounds really crazy. Nobody can see these things except me and Carol."

"Who is Carol?"

"She used to be my neighbor and she's the one who found me the other night after I took the overdose of sleep medication. She's also the one who helped me get on the phone and call you. I have been so afraid and ashamed to call you."

"This all sounds so strange. What does your doctor think?"

"He's keeping me here for who knows how long. I was in this hospital earlier in the month and he let me out. After that, I made the suicide attempt. I think he's still worried about me."

"I am too!"

"Mom, I am getting better every day. This object is helping me face my problems."

"What is this object you keep talking about?"

"Okay, it's a wooden house with twenty four little windows that looks like an advent calendar. Each day one more of the twenty-four little windows lights up and Carol and I can see what is in the window. Mostly it has been scenes from my past but the other day I saw a pretty red candle with a wreath on it and today, there was a Yule log in the window. It reminded me of the one dad used to get every year. For the first twelve days or so, only I saw these things and no one else could see them so I thought I had completely lost it. I tried to show it to my doctor and that's when he admitted me to the hospital the first time. He only saw a piece of wood, nothing else."

"Oh honey, this all sounds so strange. It doesn't make any sense to me. But you know that's interesting about you mentioning a candle because it seems just like the one I just bought yesterday! Your dad mentioned something about getting another Yule log to me just this morning."

"Really? That's amazing but it's not a coincidence I think. I can't explain any of this without sounding completely crazy. I am just so grateful that Carol can see the things too. She is a wonderful lady and I feel like I have a friend in this world again as well. I have been so lonely for so long. This calendar house has made me think a lot about the accident and losing James and the children. I have to move on and make more of my life. I want to be back in your life again. I want to see you and dad again!" Catherine began to sob.

Catherine's mother began to cry quietly on the phone too. She longed to see Catherine again as well.

"I'll talk to your father about having us get together soon. I think he will be overjoyed at seeing you. I'll call you tomorrow. Good night Catherine. Thank you again for calling."

Catherine said goodbye and hung up. She cried for a long time and finally fell asleep.

In the morning, Dr. Thomas came into the room and found Catherine asleep with reddened eyes. He was curious to inquire about the reason for the obvious crying episode. He gently woke her up and asked how she was doing. Catherine thought for a moment and then mentioned the conversation she had with her mother the previous evening. Dr. Thomas was quite pleased to hear that Catherine had finally contacted her parents again. He had encouraged this for a long time but she always came up with some excuse for not making any attempt to do so. He asked how they were doing and she spoke sadly about the news of her father's illness. Dr. Thomas was troubled by the information but tried to offer hope the best he could. Catherine said that her mother was very upset when she told her about the recent happenings, especially the suicide attempt and all that had transpired since the beginning of the month. She was encouraged that her mother mentioned trying to get together soon and was anxious to hear back from her about that today.

"This is an excellent step in your progress, Catherine," Dr. Thomas remarked.

"Dr. Thomas, it was because of Carol's encouragement. She and I are becoming good friends. I had told her about the poor relationship I have with my folks and she insisted I call them and I did!"

"So Carol has been coming back to see you?"

"Yes. I asked her to. I hope that's all right. She makes me feel better just being around her. I have finally found a friend. It's been so long."

"I am glad she has connected with you. You definitely need friendship in your life. We all do. That's another very promising sign Catherine."

She smiled and nodded. They discussed how she felt about things and Catherine seemed to dwell less and less on the problems that concerned her for so long and talked more about the future and making things better with it than she ever had in the whole time Dr. Thomas had known her. She definitely stood out from all of his other patients by how quickly she could recover and also decline.

Carol was excited to find out if Catherine's mother had called back last night as she hurried to get ready for work. Once again, she took a peak at the wooden house in the bag and looked at the fifteenth lit up window. There was a gingerbread man all decorated with a white frosting outline and raisins for buttons and a happy face. It made Carol smile when she saw it. It reminded her of childhood and making cookies with her mother. She could almost taste the ginger, molasses and spice.

When Carol showed up in Catherine's room later that day, she excitedly asked Catherine if her mother had called.

"Yes she did.  It was so hard to talk to her at first.  I can't believe it took me so long to call her.  I probably never would have had the nerve to call if you hadn't come into my life, so thank you so much for your help.  She said my dad has stomach cancer.  They weren't planning on telling me about it any time soon."

"I am so sorry to hear that.  How bad is it?"

"He's had a few chemo treatments so far but they don't know.  I just can't believe what strangers we became due to my selfishness."

"Well, there is only one way to go now and that is back up.  You can become close to them again.  It's not too late."

"I did ask if I could see them again and she said she would talk to my dad about a visit and promised to call me back."

"When you all get together soon, it can be like you never were apart if all the hearts are willing.  I will hope and pray for a rekindling of love and good will that will bring your family together again."

"Thanks.  I tried to tell my mom all about what's been happening to me since the first of the month and about the calendar house and you saving me from suicide.  I think I disappointed her again.  She asked why I was in a mental hospital and I ended up trying to explain why and telling her specifically about seeing things in the little windows.  I am pretty sure she still considers me somewhat insane."

"I can't imagine trying to tell anyone what's been going with you without sounding completely crazy. After I got that reaction from my husband the other night, it made me really scared that perhaps I was losing my mind too but I am now completely convinced things are just fine. Really, they are. Do you want to see what the calendar house has for you today?"

"Of course I do," Catherine smiled as she took the house from Carol and looked at window fifteen. "How cute is that cookie. It's making me hungry."

"I know what you mean. I'm craving gingerbread now. I wonder if the cookie has any special meaning."

"That reminds me. My mom said the candle I described seeing in the little window is just like the one she bought the other day and my dad wanted to get his traditional Yule log just yesterday. Isn't that weird?"

"So it seems like we are seeing things in the present now?"

"Perhaps we are. If that's the case, it's starting to really feel like a version of Dickens's *The Christmas Carol*, isn't it?"

"Yes, but without the ghosts! Wait a minute, could those people have been ghosts in my dream? Yikes!"

"I have no idea. This is all so strange. First of all, we both have amazing dreams; we both can see this house that shows things past and present and now, reveals to us mysteries. What could a gingerbread cookie possibly mean? Hopefully we'll be able to figure that out," Catherine uttered as she shook her head in amazement.

# *December 16ᵗʰ*

Life was getting busier in the mental hospital for Catherine as she showed good progress. In addition to more frequent visits not only from Dr. Thomas, but other medical staff as well, she began to participate in group sessions. This was a new step that Dr. Thomas had not attempted before because of her extreme anti-social behaviors. Now that she had demonstrated a longing for more social interaction with Carol, he felt she could probably handle some additional time with other patients. She was able to participate fairly well but was hesitant about sharing any specific information concerning what triggered her suicide attempt. Others in the group were more comfortable with the situation and spoke freely about their feelings and mental illness. Catherine felt overwhelmed by the prospect of sharing information with the group and she informed Dr. Thomas of this. He reassured her that there was no pressure to do so until she felt ready.

She wondered when her mother would call and continued to worry why she hadn't called on the previous day. Maybe she had changed her mind about wanting to see Catherine again. Perhaps her dad objected and now her mom didn't know what to tell her. Her worried mind only got worse hour by hour. She wondered more on the gingerbread man. Did it have some pertinent importance to her life somehow? It just seemed so absurd to think so but she reminded herself about the candle and the Yule log and how they fit perfectly together to remind her of her parents. She had considered calling her parents when she first saw the scenes with the knitting and the bicycle but fear stopped her. The additional encouragement from her new friend was all she needed to overcome that persistent fear and make contact with her parents again.

She looked forward to seeing Carol again and adding whatever showed in today's window to the gingerbread man puzzle. She was reading another book, plowing her way through the collection of novels in the therapy room, when the telephone rang in her room. It was her mother. Catherine sighed with relief.

"Hello Mom! Thank you for calling me. How are things going?"

"Fine, dear. We have been very busy at the hospital with some additional tests the doctor just ordered. I talked to your father and he said that a visit from you was very overdue. He said the sooner, the better. I told him you were in a mental hospital and wasn't sure when you would be released."

"I still have no idea when I will get out of here but Dr. Thomas says I am making remarkable progress. He had me go to a group session today for the first time. I did find it very overwhelming but somewhat helpful."

"Well, that is encouraging. It would be quite a day when we could get together again as a family, especially if we could get both girls home."

"How is Tina doing? Where is she living now? I haven't talked to her in years either."

"Frankly, I don't know. I have no idea where she is."

"What do you mean?"

"Well, she went through a terrible divorce a year or so ago. She tried to have children but was never able. Her husband became unfaithful to her and she was devastated. I tried to help but she pulled away from us just like you did after the accident and Susie's death. She up and moved away without letting us know and we do not know where she went. I haven't received a phone call or a letter since she left."

"Oh Mom, that's terrible news. I feel so bad. Poor Tina. I had no idea. I have been so caught up in my own pathetic little world, living in constant pain and anguish of soul that I never even considered that all of you might be suffering too. How can you ever forgive me?"

"I am just glad you called. It's been very difficult for your father and me. We've managed the best we can but having two daughters abandon us is very hard for us to understand. I guess there must be something genetic that is triggered by extreme stress that causes such mental and emotional breakdowns in our children. I don't know. I worry about her just like I have worried about you. I was grateful to at least get a Christmas card from you every year. I wish Tina would send something. I am hoping one of these days she will."

"I don't know what to say. Have you tried to hire someone to find her?"

"No, we haven't. I guess part of us knows she just needs some space to deal with her pain so we are waiting for her to make contact. I just hope she hasn't tried to take her life like you've tried to do."

The words stung. Catherine wept as she started to comprehend the enormous amount of pain and suffering she had caused her dear parents. They had never deserved to be treated so cruelly by the ones they loved so dearly. Catherine again apologized to her mom and said she needed to go. She hung up the phone and sat in silence, tears streaming down her face. Dr. Thomas walked in and noticed her distress.

"What is wrong, Catherine?"

She sobbed and couldn't speak. After a few minutes she managed to gain some control over her emotions and shared what she learned from her mother with Dr. Thomas.

"Dr. Thomas, I am a terrible person!" Catherine yelled.

"Catherine, you have a mental illness. You are not a terrible person."

"How could I have been so thoughtless and cruel to my family? I abandoned my little sister. She had to go through all of that pain alone. Now she's gone and who knows what she's dealing with?"

Dr. Thomas didn't respond but realized Catherine had come to herself. She had passed a significant milestone of being able to look beyond her problems and consider others. He had been working with her on this goal for a long time. The light was beginning to break through the clouds of darkness that had engulfed her mind for many years. Dr. Thomas felt very hopeful for Catherine. He continued to offer his counsel and encouraged her to attend the afternoon group session. He also suggested using a journal to write down her feelings as another form of therapy.

For once, Catherine took his advice and requested a pen and a notebook.

Maurice with his sunshine helped lift her spirits when he stopped by with lunch.

"I can see you have been crying again, Miss Catherine. What's wrong?"

"Oh I just talked to my mom and found out some sad news about my sister."

"I 'm sorry to hear that. Is she okay?"

"I don't know. I don't know where she is and neither do my parents. I feel so much to blame for all of this."

Maurice stopped smiling for a minute. He got very serious looking and finally said, "The love between families is one of the most powerful forces on earth. You are feeling that right now. It'll work out for you. You'll see."

"What do you mean?"

"My family's love for me is mighty powerful and I know it helped rescue me from a bad place. A real miracle happened. Turned me around, turned me toward God."

"What happened to you?"

"I was messed up real bad. Drugs. Bad people. My heart was so low and I felt lost. Well, it seemed my family they were praying real hard for me. One day, this fellow found me, lying in the alley, half dead. He was real kind to me. Took me in. Fed me.

Had the best smile in the world. He said some mighty powerful words to me that I will never forget. He told me that I had some real special things to do with my life, that I had a big heart that could just shine on others and help them along, but the best thing he said to me was that I had a family that loved me so much that they prayed for an angel to come along and rescue me from the hell that I was in. I swear right at that moment, he did look like an angel. His face glowed like he was full of light and my heart just about burst with all the warmth and love that I was feeling."

"That's amazing."

"I was never the same after that. I promised my friend whose name was Matthias that I would get out of the hell I was living in. He showed me where I could go to get clean from drugs and put my life back together and then he disappeared. It was hard but I did it because I never felt alone after that. I knew God was there helping me all along the way. When I finally got back to see my family again, it was pure joy. I thanked them for praying for me. The love of family is mighty powerful. You'll get a miracle, Miss Catherine. I believe that."

"Thank you Maurice for sharing that with me. I feel comforted and more hopeful now."

Maurice beamed a magnificent smile and she could feel the love of his big heart just shining upon her. She could feel that warmth even after he left her room. She looked at the lunch he brought but didn't get too excited about that. She picked at the lunch that consisted of a cheese sandwich, carrot sticks and a bowl of tomato soup.

Catherine wrote a lot down in the notebook by the time Carol showed up. She wrote about what Maurice had shared with her and how he was like Carol, bringing sunshine to help melt the winter away in her heart. Once again, she brought some lunch to share with Catherine.

"Oh Carol, it's so good to see you again. You bring sunlight into my life every time I see you! Thank you for bringing lunch again. You didn't have to do that again. You are so kind."

"It's nothing. I have to eat anyways and this is a great way to spend my lunch break. I notice you've been crying. Are you okay?"

"I heard from my mom again this morning. She said my dad wanted to see me again but she also said that my younger sister Tina got divorced and now they don't know where she is. I feel just terrible about everything. I have been so horrible to my family. I just never considered their feelings all this time."

Catherine started to weep again. Carol reached out and offered a hug for comfort.

"I just had all of this pent up anger for so long. I really don't even remember what made me so mad except that it had to do something with Susie's death. All I know is that I didn't want anything to do with them anymore. What a stupid person I was for thinking that and then cutting off ties with them. I have been so cruel to my poor parents. I can't believe what they have had to endure all these years. Now Tina is doing the same thing to them! I need to try to help her. I just don't know where she could be."

"Were you ever close with your sister?"

"For a long time we were very close. After I got married we kind of drifted apart but still managed to stay in touch. I just remember praying hard as a little girl for a baby sister and she came right before Christmas. That's why she is called Christina. We called her Tina for short. Oh, how I miss her! Her birthday is in a few days, on the twenty second."

"Is the little window with the baby cradle in it about your sister?"

"Yes. I remember that Christmas so well. I was about five years old. I worked very hard at being a good big sister. What happened to me? I am the worst big sister imaginable now."

"No you're not. That bridge can be repaired too. It's not too late. You and your sister still love each other. Here, look at the calendar house today. It'll help get your mind back on solving our mystery."

Catherine took the wooden house, which shimmered brighter than ever today, and peered into the window with the number sixteen painted on it and she saw a bell. It was beautiful and reminded her of the bell ornaments that were on her family's Christmas tree when she was a little girl. She liked to shake the tree branches and hear the bells jingle. She also loved to play with the little snowmen and bird ornaments on the tree and build little nests out of the aluminum tinsel that hung in shiny streams all over the tree.

"That's interesting, but what could a gingerbread man and a bell mean?"

"Would it have anything to do with your sister, perhaps? Did she like gingerbread cookies or bells?"

"I think she liked gingerbread cookies really well. In fact I remember one year getting a whole box of them from her, with ribbons in little holes at the top of the head so we could hang them on the Christmas tree. My kids loved them. They were all gone off the tree and eaten before Santa Claus could help himself to one."

Carol chuckled at the memory. "That sounds so fun. Do you think she still makes them? Maybe she baked and decorated some yesterday, wherever she might be."

"I think you are right. The more I think about it, Tina's favorite holiday tradition was baking cookies. But how does the bell fit into all of this? I hope we can get another useful clue tomorrow."

"I love solving mysteries. This is so fun."

"It is. I just wished I knew where Tina was now. I could at least help my parents that way. I need the miracle Maurice was talking about."

"Who is Maurice?"

"He's the orderly that delivers my meals sometimes. He is a large black man with an incredible smile and a kind heart. He shared some encouraging words with me a little before you showed up today. He was promising me a miracle about my family and I sure need one to help find Tina."

"Well, you have your miracle already in this calendar house and by using it, you will soon know about your sister. In the meantime, don't punish yourself too hard. You had to deal with pain that most people will never have to even think about. What happened was your way of dealing with it. Everyone deals with pain differently. You just chose to go inside for a long time and now you coming out again. It's so exciting to see the change in you in just a short amount of time. I really think you are getting well."

"I think Dr. Thomas is feeling a lot better about me. Hopefully I can get out of this place soon. Thanks for the delicious lunch and coming to see me again. Do you work tomorrow?"

"Yes, with the Christmas shopping season almost at its peak, I am putting more hours and days at the store. It's crazy there. I like being able to get away for a little while and come to a little peace and quiet here in the hospital."

"I am just so grateful you are willing to come see me. I can't thank you enough."

Carol smiled and gave Catherine another hug.

"See you tomorrow!"

# *December 17th*

It seemed like the longer Catherine remained in the hospital the smaller her four walls became. She looked forward to getting out of her room at every chance she could. Dr. Thomas took this as another positive sign of her recovery. When she had her previous stays in the hospital, Catherine was always more content to remain in her room as much as possible and be away from other people. Hospital staff would persistently encourage her to participate in whatever was available for group therapy but Catherine preferred isolation. The doctors would always have to see Catherine in her room.

Dr. Thomas attributed this remarkable change to the daily visits from Carol. Catherine's countenance was the most significant difference that he could notice. She was starting to look happy. She smiled more. This morning she had participated again in group therapy but this time she spoke up for a few minutes. It surprised even Catherine. She didn't say very much except to add a comment after another patient finished talking about her suicide attempt. Catherine merely mentioned that she didn't think about doing it much beforehand until she went to get some sleep medicine and instead of taking the normal dose, she poured out the entire bottle and swallowed them all.

The desire to connect with other people seemed to be growing each day. She attempted to speak with another person after the group session was over which she had never considered doing before. Dr. Thomas noticed this and went to speak with her.

"Catherine, I must say that you are making tremendous strides here. I just became aware that you participated in the group session today and just now, I saw you talking to another patient. This is just wonderful! You look happier. What is going on with you to bring about this amazing turnaround?"

"Carol. She's been by to see me every day. Ever since I called my parents the other day, I have been feeling better about everything. However, I am very worried about my sister who is missing. I told you about that, didn't I?"

"Yes, you've mentioned your sister to me. What exactly happened?"

"I guess she went through a terrible divorce and then had a nervous breakdown. It sounded a lot like what I went through.

She's moved away from my parent's town and they do not know where she went. I feel so bad for them, especially since they already went through all that with me the first time."

"Do you think your sister has suicidal tendencies as well?"

"I don't know and that's why I am so worried. I can't do anything about it because no one knows where she might be now. It's a terrible mess and I feel partly to blame. I have been so selfish by cutting myself off from everyone all these years. I only worried about myself."

"And now you feel responsible for your sister?"

"Yes, I do. I need to talk to her again. I am her big sister. I need to look out for her like I used to!"

Dr. Thomas stood staring at his patient in amazement. Hearing her once again mention concern for the wellbeing of another showed him that Catherine indeed had a major emotional breakthrough. She had never been able to express concern for anybody but herself in the whole time she had been his patient. He excitedly excused himself to go discuss the case with other doctors in the hospital.

Catherine headed for the therapy room to do another puzzle and kill time before Carol's visit. She was too restless to sit and read this morning. The hospital was becoming more prison like every day. She longed for freedom. What would she do when she was finally released? At this point, the idea of returning to work seemed more unappealing than ever. She had lived a meager existence for such a long time and now began to yearn for more in her life.

She couldn't wait to see what new clue might be in today's little window. Hopefully it might reveal enough information about her sister to answer the question burning in her heart about her sister's current whereabouts. She looked around the room. She once again noticed the Christmas decorations put up haphazardly on the walls and how they looked old and faded. She hadn't decorated for Christmas in many years. She didn't even own any decorations anymore. Suddenly she felt the desire to decorate, perhaps only a little, this year for the holiday. Maybe she would even get a small little tree. She wanted to get Carol a gift. This too was the first time in many years that she felt the desire to celebrate Christmas by giving a gift to someone. She had in the past-avoided parties and any celebrations and passed the holiday by reading or watching a good movie. The spirit of Christmas was gently resting upon her awakening soul.

Catherine noticed other people in the room attempting to put together a large jigsaw puzzle and she decided to join them.

"Can I help?" She asked.

"Oh, sure," a lady in a wheelchair answered, "I am having trouble finding the pieces with the church steeple in it."

Catherine sat down and started scanning the various pieces for images of a steeple but quickly her eyes were caught up by the various brick patterns from buildings on some of the pieces. It intrigued her and also reminded her of somewhere she had been in the past. She decided to collect those pieces and try to assemble them. This occupied her mind thoroughly so that the time passed quickly and suddenly Carol showed up at the door.

"Hi Catherine," she called. Catherine looked up and smiled. She stood up and took a long look at the partially assembled puzzle and still felt curious at where she had seen these brick buildings before.

"What are you working on?" Carol walked over and studied the puzzle, "What a beautiful little town. I love New England towns in the fall. Look at those leaves, such brilliant colors of orange and red!"

Catherine looked up at her and wondered. Maybe she had been to this town before. It did remind her of the lovely town she visited many years ago and met her husband. She was grateful for the therapy this time had provided. She continued to relax more day by day and enjoyed the simple opportunities around her even in the mental hospital.

"Well, what does it show?" Catherine asked Carol as they headed towards her room.

"It's even stranger than yesterday. Today there is a holiday ham in the window! What do you think of that?" Carol asked as she pulled out the calendar house once they were inside the room with the door closed. To her amazement, there was a ham in the window.

"How strange is that?" Catherine asked Carol.

"This is really weird. First there was a gingerbread cookie, then a bell and now a ham. Did you sister like ham too?"

"I have no idea. We never had ham that I could remember on Christmas. I remember having beef roasts the most."

"Well, what do bells and hams have in common then?"

"Beats me. Let's see, a bell and a ham. I have no idea what they could possible mean. Oh, this is really frustrating today!"

The ladies sat in silence for a few minutes trying to rack their brains for a solution.

"A bell and ham," Catherine repeated over a few times quietly and then she declared, "I know!"

"What?" Carol asked excitedly.

"Bellingham! You know, Bellingham, Washington? Maybe that's where my sister is!"

"Really?"

"I'm not sure but I sort of remember my mother telling me that Tina had a very close friend she met at college who lived in Bellingham, Washington who Tina wanted to go visit. I don't know if she ever did. That was years ago."

"Would your mother know?"

"I don't know if she would but it is worth finding out. Can I borrow your phone again?"

"Sure."

Carol handed the phone to an excited Catherine. She dialed the number again and Catherine's mother answered.

"Hi Mom!"

"Hello Catherine. How are you doing today?"

"I'm doing so much better. I have a question about Tina. Do you remember anything about Tina's friend from college that she wanted to go visit? Didn't she live in Bellingham, Washington?"

"I think that sounds right. Why do you ask?"

"I think that is where we might find Tina."

"How did you figure that out?"

"Oh, Mom, it's that strange calendar house again. It's acting like a crystal ball but doing it like a puzzle with pieces that have to be fit together. There was a bell in the window yesterday and a ham today and I put them together and it reminded me of Bellingham. It's really possible that she might have gone to stay with her friend there, who knows. Did she ever go stay there before?"

"Yes, but that was years ago. She stayed for a week or two. I can't remember."

"Do you have the friend's name or address anywhere perhaps?"

"I'll have to look. I might have written it down in my old address book. I think that it is in the attic. I'll go look and I will call you back."

"Thanks, Mom."

Catherine gently closed the cell phone, handed it back to Carol and thanked her.

"This is amazing you know. What if it's the right place and you find your sister?"

"It will be the miracle Maurice promised and I will be so grateful. I want to talk to her so bad. There is so much I want to say but most of all I want to tell I am so sorry for cutting her out of my life."

"Where is Bellingham? I've heard of it but I have no idea where I would find it."

"I think its north of Seattle, Washington, pretty close to the Canadian border."

"I wonder if it gets pretty cold there in the winter. Maybe it's more like Seattle."

Carol changed the subject to ask Catherine what her plans were once she got released from the hospital. Catherine said she didn't want to go back to her old job but she wasn't sure about anything yet.

The cellphone ringing interrupted the conversation. Carol handed the phone back to Catherine.

"Hello, Mom? Did you find it?"

"I think so."

# *December 18th*

When Catherine talked to her mother the previous day she discovered that Tina's friend was Sally Baxter and she had a phone number and address listed for her. Catherine anxiously copied down the information and promised her mom that she would try to make contact a soon as she could and let her know. She tried the number but no one answered so she told Carol that she would try again to call it the next day when Carol returned.

Catherine kept busy reading and working on crossword puzzles between therapy sessions to make the time pass quickly. At 2:00 PM, Carol once again slipped into the room and gave the calendar house to Catherine to examine.

"Look at what is in the window today," Carol declared excitedly.

Catherine recognized at once the little Christmas tree necklace. "I remember this," She said softly. "I gave it to my friend Peggy Swanson for Christmas years ago."

"Well, that's strange. I thought everything shown in the windows now had to do with the present."

"You're right. I wondered that myself. I should ask my mom about Peggy when I call her. Maybe she knows where Peggy is. I lost touch with her years ago after the accident too. All of these wonderful people were just flicked aside by me like they didn't matter anymore. How could I have been so cruel?" Catherine agonized.

Carol encouraged Catherine to try reaching her sister again. When she called the number, someone answered this time but there wasn't anyone by the name of Sally living there. She then called information and asked for Sally Baxter. There was no listing for anyone by that name so she asked the operator if she had any phone number listed for a given address. There was a number listed publicly for Sally's old address. When she called this number, there was no one by the name of Sally Baxter living there. Catherine felt discouraged but before hanging up she asked the lady who answered the phone if she might know the whereabouts of Sally Baxter who used to live at that residence. After a moment, the person responded that they knew a Baxter family in town and they might know of her. Catherine waited for a few minutes while the phone number was retrieved. Catherine thanked the lady for her kindness and hung up.

This time Catherine was successful in reaching the Baxter residence. Catherine discovered by talking to the man on the phone that Sally Baxter was now Sally Baxter Green and she was still living in Bellingham. Catherine explained who she was and how she was trying to reach her sister Tina and that Sally might know her whereabouts. The man introduced himself as Dave Baxter, Sally's uncle. He gave her Sally's cell phone number. Catherine was amazed at the success she was having.

She could hardly contain her excitement when she called Sally and told her who she was.

"Hello, is Sally there?"

"Yes, this is Sally."

"Hi Sally, my name is Catherine Daley and I am Tina Spear's sister. I was wondering if you would know how I could reach her. "

"You are the sister she hasn't heard from in years?"

Catherine paused at the painful question and then answered with an embarrassed yes.

"Well, she'll be surprised to hear from you. Do you know she lives here in Bellingham?"

"I was hoping that she did. I just talked to my mother and she had no idea where Tina had moved. I remembered that she had a good friend in Bellingham, Washington that she once stayed with for a little while. My mom found your name and address in an old address book. After a few tries of different phone numbers, I called your uncle and he gave me your new number. I am so grateful I found you and maybe you know how I can reach Tina."

"She and I have stayed close all these years. Tina came out to visit me about a year ago after her terrible divorce. She had a dreadful time emotionally and just wanted to get away from everything for a while. She's had some regrets about what she did but she's working through her issues and getting some medical help too now, which seems to be helping somewhat. It's a nice town and she decided to stay. She found a decent job and an apartment, not too far from where my husband and I live. I see her a lot. I can give you her new phone number."

"Thank you so much! You've been such a good friend to her. I just wish I hadn't been so thoughtless all these years. I cut off my family and tried to pretend that no one existed anymore but me. It's a terrible way to live. I wish I had been there for her. I am glad Tina had you to get the support she needed. Nervous breakdowns do weird things to people. I am still dealing with many issues from mine a long time ago."

"Tina told me what happened. I am so sorry for you. I can't even imagine how you even survived as well as you did."

"I barely survived. I hid the pain. I couldn't deal with it. However I have been forced in recent weeks to deal with it again and that has led me to contact my parents, then you in the hopes of trying to reconnect with Tina again as hard as it is. I hope she'll forgive me. I hope my parents can forgive me too."

"Well, you've all been through a lot. She should be home right now. I think she's working later today. Good luck. It was nice to talk to you."

Sally gave Catherine Tina's new phone number and hung up. Catherine looked over at Carol and smiled enthusiastically at her.

"This is so incredible. It's really a miracle. That calendar house knows these things but I don't know how. It's kind of eerie but at the same time, it is so cool!"

"It's got heavenly power, that's all. God knows everything and there are no coincidences when He's involved."

Catherine smiled when Carol said that. Tina answered when Catherine dialed her phone number.

"Hello?'

"Tina?"

"Yes, who is this?"

"It's Catherine, your sister."

There was a long pause.

"Catherine?"

"Yes. It's me."

"Oh my gosh, I can't believe it! How on earth did you find me?"

"That's a long story. How are you?"

"I am doing okay. How about you?"

"I am doing much better. Oh Tina, I am so sorry. I have been so horrible to you. I wished I could go back and do everything so different! I'm your only big sister and I have hurt you so much. How can you ever forgive me for what I did to you?"

"I kind of just got used to not having a sister anymore. It was like you died too along with your family in the accident. But that was then and this is now and we all have to move on. But you know, I have been thinking about you a lot lately. I am really glad you called."

"I just went off the deep end and I have been in a gulf of misery ever since. My depression got really bad. I avoided people as much as I could. What was I thinking? I even tried to kill myself twice."

"Wow. I am glad you weren't successful. I have had a lot of depression myself and I had those thoughts of suicide too but I never acted on them. I didn't deal with what Jason did to me very well."

"I was so sad to hear about that. Mom told me."

"How is she doing?"

"Not too well, I'm afraid. She is very upset about not knowing where you moved to and that dad has stomach cancer."

"What? You're kidding. Oh my goodness, that's terrible! How long has he had it?"

"They've known about six months now and the prognosis is still uncertain."

"Poor mom and dad. I've been so selfish not letting them know where I went. I guess I just went a bit crazy like you did and cut myself off from them and everything for a while."

"They can probably never understand why we did that either. They certainly never deserved it. How can we make it up to them?"

"I will call mom right away and apologize. We need to go home, Catherine, and see them!"

"You're right. We should do that. However, I'm stuck in this mental hospital right now and I am not sure when I will be released."

"Why are you in a mental hospital? Is it because of your suicide attempt?"

"Yes, I'm afraid."

"Well, it sounds like you are making some good progress both mentally and emotionally."

"I guess so. I finally overcame my fear of calling mom and dad. My friend Carol has helped me so much to do this."

"Who is Carol?"

"She was my neighbor, found me after I took an overdose and she saved me from death both times!"

"Wow. She sounds like an amazing person. I want to meet her."

"Yeah, you would really like her," Catherine smiled at Carol who was getting restless to get back to work.

"Well, I am going to go home to see them for Christmas, if they will have me back after what I did to them. You should do that too if you can."

"I will try. I have to go Tina but I will call you soon. I am going to call mom now and let her know I found you. It's so great to talk to you again. Thank you for being my sister."

"Bye Catherine. Thanks again for calling me."

Catherine dialed her parent's number again.

"Hi Mom."

"Catherine?"

"Yes, it's me. I found her Mom. I talked to Tina!"

"Oh that's wonderful. So she's living in Bellingham, Washington? How is she doing?"

"Better. She's going to call you. She's sorry to have done that to you and Dad. We are both worthless daughters who don't deserve such wonderful parents."

"I'm just so grateful to know you are both okay. I have been praying hard for this moment for a long time."

"Mom, I was wondering if you remember my friend Peggy Swanson? Do you know where she might be now? I lost touch with her too. The calendar house has a little Christmas tree necklace in today's window, just like the one I once gave to Peggy. It reminded me of her."

"I want to see that calendar house of yours! It is truly remarkable. It must be from God."

"I think you're right, Mom. There is no other way to explain it and what has happened to me. He has helped me so much. I need to find out about Peggy if you know anything about her."

"Well, she just recently moved back in with her parents. They still live here in town. She never did get married. I don't think you even know that she had a bad fall about five years ago and injured her spine pretty bad. She's confined to a wheelchair now."

"Oh, that is so sad. Here is another person who has suffered a great deal and I was so heartless to cut her out of my life like I did my dear parents and sister. I hope I can see her again. I want to come see you and Dad and so does Tina. We want to come for Christmas. Would that be alright?"

"For Christmas? That would be so wonderful! I can't wait to go tell your father."

"I hope I can come. It all depends on when I get released from this hospital. I'll do whatever it takes Mom. I want to be there!" Then Catherine heard herself say something she hadn't said in years, "I love you, Mom!"

There was a long pause and then her mom said in return, "I love you too, Catherine. Thank you dear for finding Tina and for calling me."

After Catherine handed the phone back to Carol she sat down on the bed in total amazement and started to cry. The tears were now ones of joy. Her heart felt warm and full of light.

"It's a complete miracle. Wow. I am so happy for you Catherine. You did it! I am so proud of you," Carol declared. "I'm sorry but I have to go now. Things are just crazy at the store."

"Thank you so much for everything. I couldn't have done any of it without your help," Catherine stood up and gave her dear friend a warm embrace of gratitude before she left.

# December 19th

Catherine felt true comfort in her heart for the first time in years.  Her life was getting immensely better.  She had just built two bridges to reconnect herself to the people who mattered most to her now, her parents and sister.  Her life felt new and promising and she gladly welcomed it.  The sun was shining outside on freshly fallen snow.  It sparkled like diamonds and looked so beautiful that she wanted to be outside to enjoy it.  She was anxious to begin a new life outside the dreary institution that held her prisoner.  The dark and confining world she had built for herself now seemed like a bad dream she just woke up from.  After all these years, spring had finally arrived in her heart.  Sweet forgiveness had melted away the hardened feelings that had clung to her heart so heavily as to pull her down into the depths of extreme despair and loneliness.

She walked briskly up and down the halls, smiling at everyone she met and saying warm hellos. The hospital staff began to inquire among themselves the reasons for this enormous change in Catherine's demeanor and personality. They were used to her looking down and avoiding people's glances and greetings. She paused at a window where sunshine was beaming through and lifted her face and closed her eyes to experience the brightness and warmth it provided. Inside, she felt the light too.

Catherine looked forward to seeing Dr. Thomas for the first time in a long time. She was so excited to share with him her wonderful news of finding her sister and being able to go back and spend Christmas with her family. Surely he would consider her release today or tomorrow. The old Catherine of yesteryear was resurfacing. She was still shy but the feelings of happiness she felt in her heart now made her want to talk to people again. She went to the morning therapy session and surprised the participants by her increased involvement in the discussions. She actually enjoyed the session for the very first time.

When she came back to her room, she found Maurice delivering her lunch with his usual upbeat attitude. Today she joined him in his happiness.

"Hi Maurice! How are you today?" Catherine greeted him excitedly.

"Why Miss Catherine, what a pleasure it is to see you with a beautiful smile today. I can see the clouds are gone and the sun is shining in your heart. Your eyes have a sparkle in them," Maurice said with his usual chuckle. His laughter was contagious today more than usual and Catherine felt herself laughing along with him. She hadn't felt the desire to laugh in a long time and now it felt so good.

"I called my sister yesterday. I hadn't talked to her in years. I think she's forgiven me and my parents have forgiven me too. I am so glad. I am hoping to spend Christmas with them."

"Why that's wonderful news! Doesn't it just feel fine to let go of all those old bad feelings and let God's light back into your heart? Your family still loves you and now you know it. Didn't I tell you they would?"

"Yes. Thank you for your encouragement. You said I would get a miracle about my family and I did. You were like a ray of sunshine every day to me. No matter what you've gone through in your life Maurice, all that bad stuff, you are happy. I want to be like that too from now on."

"You will Miss Catherine, you will. Keep your heart open, love those around you and you can always be happy. There's always someone to help every day. There's always somebody to lift with your smile and kind words."

"Well you certainly helped lift me up out of despair and my friend Carol too. God sent me two angels this Christmas season and a very special gift!" Catherine said earnestly. Maurice just chuckled.

"Well, Miss Catherine, God takes pity on us and sends us exactly what we need to get going right again. It looks like you might get out of here very soon and I wish you well. If I don't see you again, have a blessed and happy Christmas with your wonderful family."

"I will. You have a very Merry Christmas too."

The words lifted Catherine's heart. She hadn't wished anyone a merry Christmas in many years. It felt absolutely marvelous.

It wasn't long before Dr. Thomas showed up for his morning visit.

"Hi Dr. Thomas!" exclaimed Catherine cheerfully.

A startled Dr. Thomas quickly smiled and responded with an enthusiastic hello.

"My we are looking quite chipper this morning aren't we?"

"Oh, yes. I feel wonderful today!"

"Well, that's good news."

"Speaking of good news, I managed to find my sister yesterday and we talked. It was totally amazing how I was able to locate her. That was a miracle in itself I think She's really forgiven me for pushing her out of my life for so long. I have let go of all of that stupid anger towards my family and everyone who hurt me in the past. We are all ready to finally move on. She told me that she's planning on spending Christmas with mom and dad. I want to be there too."

"Catherine that is just marvelous. Since you've been here you've made contact with both your parents and your sister?"

"Yes. I just wished it hadn't taken me so long to do it. I don't know how much time my dad might have left now. My poor parents, they have been through so much. My sister has too. I have been so cruel to all of them, so selfish."

"Now Catherine, don't be too hard on yourself. Perhaps the hardest kind of forgiveness is learning to forgive one's self."

"But Dr. Thomas, how can I make it up to them? How can I undo all the hurt I caused?"

"Just go forward, Catherine. Focus on today and don't dwell on things that you can't change, like your past. There are good times ahead for you. There is joy to be found in living your life. There are still wonderful times to share with your folks. Just look at how much progress you've made in just six short days! You've reconnected with the world around you. You made a new friend and reestablished family relationships again. I've just got to make sure that your mental state stabilizes through all of this and that you don't slip into another depression. I think we are finding the right medications finally."

Catherine smiled at Dr. Thomas who seemed to only perceive things through his medical point of view. To him the healing he was seeing in Catherine was the result of the drugs interacting properly in her brain and the counseling, therapy sessions and a new friendship that helped her gain the proper perspective in dealing with her emotions.

While all of these things were most likely contributing to Catherine's increase in wellbeing, the catalyst for change was the miracle of two human beings interacting with each other, experiencing the unexplainable inside a beautiful wooden object of unknown origin and being able to validate one another.

It was the quiet workings of the heart that was helping Catherine to move on from her tragic past. Photographs of family members had long since vanished from her life because they were too painful a reminder of love lost. She had carefully tried to rid herself of any painful tokens and pictures of her past, prevented any further pain by avoiding people in general and lived a cold sterilized life centered on the mundane. She had successfully done so until the little house with windows showed up at her doorstep only two weeks earlier. Just like photographs, it had provided enough visual evidence to conjure up the very deepest memories and unleash pent up emotions that had been tucked away in the mind and heart carefully for many years.

The true therapy to her heart and mind was from being reminded of what had once been. Catherine was becoming aware again of how much she still loved her family both living and dead and realizing her family had not abandoned her when they died, that they were close by if only in her dreams. It was as if they were deeply aware of her prolonged suffering and had concocted this plan of providing the calendar house to nudge her back to a more happy and productive life and to help her reconnect with her living loved ones. The long awaited healing had arrived and now it was time for Catherine to progress on to better things. It was a time for family again with her parents and sister who needed her love and support dearly.

Catherine's happy demeanor and positive answers to Dr. Thomas's questions seemed to further convince him that a medical release from the hospital should be considered and sooner than expected. He consulted with other medical staff. They were fascinated with Catherine's rapid progress and curious to know the possible causes for her amazing improvement. Normally the road back from suicide is a long struggle to regain the will to improve and succeed, much like Catherine's journey after her first suicide attempt. He mentioned briefly about a connection she had made with the woman who had found her unconscious in that they had similar dreams but didn't want to elaborate too much further on the matter. He emphasized the importance of establishing relationships with others when a person feels disconnected from the world, which sometimes leads to a suicide attempt. He did mention to his colleagues that Catherine no longer insisted that the piece of wood was anything but a piece of wood and he felt that this was a significant change along with her improved mental state.

Catherine anxiously awaited Carol's return later that afternoon. She was curious what object the calendar house would reveal today and whom she would be reminded of by it. The past six days had dramatically changed her life. She looked forward with great anticipation at seeing her sister again and her parents. She felt sad about Peggy but hopeful she would be able to see her again and reestablish a very old friendship. Dr. Thomas did allude somewhat to a possible release soon from the hospital if things continued to proceed well for Catherine. She felt very hopeful about it and tried her best to be patient.

Finally Carol showed up but it was quite late in the day.

"I'm sorry to be so late today. I just couldn't get away from the store until now. I have family coming to stay tonight so I have to leave quickly but here's the house. I'm not sure what it means but it's more than an object. It looks like a Christmas scene again. Does it look familiar to you?"

Catherine took the calendar house and peered carefully at the nineteenth window. It showed a scene of the front door of a house. There was a beautiful large wreath on the door, decorated with fruit, pinecones and red berries. It was quite colorful. The door was a dark red color. Catherine was very puzzled by it. It didn't remind her of anything she had ever seen before.

"So who does this wreath remind you of?" Carol asked. Catherine shook her head.

"No one? No old boyfriend you need to go meet again or something?" Carol chuckled.

"Very funny," Catherine answered and then laughed at the thought, "I have never seen anything exactly like this in my life. Now what could that mean? It's a very interesting wreath. I would have remembered seeing this wreath if I'd seen it before. Maybe it belongs to someone I know here in town that I need to talk to. The problem is that I don't really know anyone here in town except you, Dr. Thomas, my boss Frank Barton and a lady at work named Alice. Wow. That's really pathetic, isn't it? I have lived here all these years and I only really know four people by name. I have a lot of catching up to do."

"When do you think you are going to get out of here? I'm planning on having a party at my house tomorrow night. That would give you a chance to meet my husband and some of my other friends. I think you would like them. My mother, daughter and grandson will be there too. I really want you to meet them."

"I'm hopeful it will be soon. I would love to go to your party. Dr. Thomas is running out of reasons for keeping me here. Maybe if I mention the party tomorrow night and that I think it would do me good to go, he will have no choice but to send me packing. Oh, how I want to get out of here!"

"I sure hope so. In the meantime, think what the wreath might mean. What mystery do we need to solve now?"

Just then Dr. Thomas walked into the room, which surprised both women. They had forgotten to close the door to the room. Catherine was sure he would notice the wooden house but she didn't realize that Carol had already slipped it into the bag as she was preparing to leave.

"Well hello Carol. How are you?"

"Hi Dr. Thomas. I am doing well."

"I hear you've been coming to see Catherine every day. You seem to be very instrumental in her amazing recovery. She desperately needed your special friendship so thank you for all you have done to help her."

"Well, it's been a real pleasure for me to get to know Catherine better. She's a wonderful person and now a cherished friend of mine. We share a very special bond."

"You've helped more than I could have ever imagined. Are you leaving now?" Dr. Thomas asked as he watched Carol put her coat on.

"Yes, I'm sorry but I need to get home before my family shows up. It's wonderful to see you again, Dr. Thomas. Have a merry Christmas."

Both Catherine and Dr. Thomas said goodbye to Carol as she left and then Catherine looked excitedly at Dr. Thomas as she thought about Carol's party invitation.

# *December 20ᵗʰ*

Catherine woke up and racked her brain about the where she might have seen a wreath that looked like the one in yesterday's little window. She hoped in time that it would make some sense to her. After Carol left yesterday, Catherine pleaded with Dr. Thomas about releasing her from the hospital. She reminded him how important it was that she be with her family for Christmas considering her father's sickness. She had also mentioned the invitation to Carol's party and how she really wanted to go. This really surprised Dr. Thomas, as he could not imagine his patient participating in anything like a holiday party. The change in Catherine was becoming quite dramatic.

When she sounded so excited about the party he realized she was probably ready to be dismissed from her hospital stay. He still worried about the possibility of a sudden decline from her as the previous week had revealed. Catherine had become the most unpredictable person he had ever met. Yet there was a new light emanating from her, a new effervescence in her countenance, speech and her goals. He had to give her a chance to be back in the real world to test out this new change in her personality and see if she would be able to manage well. It was like an experiment to send her out of the controlled safe environment of the hospital. Would she turn to the support of her new friend Carol and lean on her when things turned difficult again? At that point Dr. Thomas felt hopeful enough about Catherine that he decided to release her the next morning. He was also pleased that she continually seemed to decline any sleep medication at least for the past three days. This was a positive trend. Perhaps she would need less narcotic medication from now on as she was finding solace in other things. Dr. Thomas left her room and said he would consider the possibility of an early release.

Catherine looked hopeful when Dr. Thomas showed up in her room. She was now dressed and ready to leave at his say so.

"I hesitate to have a suicide patient discharged so early but you're really ready to leave this place, aren't you?"

"Oh yes! I can't wait to leave. I know it's only been a week since my suicide attempt but I feel so much better about everything, it's just amazing. Thank you so much for everything you've done to help me."

Dr. Thomas thought back to just a few days previous when Catherine refused to even speak with him and now she was bubbling over with kindness towards him.

"I just wish all my patients felt that way. Thank you. You are most amazing to me. It was just a few days ago you were so full of venom and now look at you. I can't believe this. It's quite miraculous. You are one for the record books I think."

Catherine just smiled at the comment.

"Well, I can't think of any reason to keep you here any longer but I have to tell you that part of me is still very worried about your leaving so soon. You must promise me, and this time you must keep your promise, to check in with me often, no matter how you are feeling."

"I will Dr. Thomas, I promise. This time I won't disregard you like I did last week. I guess it was just losing my job like that sent me crashing down. At that point I didn't care about anything or anyone. Life just seemed so pointless. But I really don't feel that way anymore. Isn't that a miracle? And another thing that's amazing is that I don't care about that job anymore at all."

"You don't? What are you going to do?"

"I'm not sure. I'm going to go back east to see my family and really celebrate Christmas with them for the first time in a very long time. I'll decide what I am going to do after that. I just feel like there is so much more to my life and I want to find out what it is. I've been living in such a cold dark cave for so long; I'm ready to leave it."

"Well that is a pretty accurate description of your life as long as I have known you. I guess all I have done for you was to help you survive in it. You had to decide when it was time for you to leave it. Welcome back to the world, Catherine."

"Thank you. I'm so glad to be back. Now I'm so ready to leave the hospital. When can I go?"

"As soon as I complete your paperwork."

"How do I get home? I don't have my car here. Maybe Carol can pick me up? That probably wouldn't work because she has her family staying with her now. I could call a taxi. That should work."

Catherine kept herself occupied until the paperwork was completed and then got into the waiting taxi. This time she thoroughly enjoyed the sights of the season around the town on the way home and she became excited at the prospects of celebrating Christmas again. When the taxi pulled up in front of the little home on Sycamore Street, she sighed at the plainness of it. The house was an off-white color with light brown trim and door; it had no Christmas decorations of any sort and just looked bleak among the snowdrifts. She looked around at all of the other homes on the street and enjoyed seeing beautiful wreaths and other decorations on some of the houses. One wreath in particular caught her attention on a house across the street. It looked very similar to the wreath she saw the previous day in the calendar house.

At once she was reminded about the mystery of the door wreath in the nineteenth window.

"I wonder if it has anything to do with the neighbor across the street. The wreath on that door looks so similar and the door is even red. Maybe I need to go over and meet that person for some reason," Catherine began to feel nervous. "I don't know what to do."

Suddenly the need to talk to Carol overwhelmed her. She would know what to do. It was hard to enter the dark lonely house again. Now her small dreary home really seemed to be the dark cave she had described to Dr. Thomas earlier. She looked around the tiny living room at the recliner, couch and television console. The furniture looked so drab like it came straight from a second hand store. It probably had but she never thought about it like this before. The rental house had been furnished when she moved in. She had thought about buying a house every so often but she didn't want the permanence of home ownership. She realized that she owned very little. The house that she and James owned had long since been sold and much of the money from it went towards paying the medical debt of Susie's extended hospitalization along with some of the insurance money she received after James's death. She had been diligent about stashing away most of her income and now she had a sizeable nest egg, which would present her some significant options for the future.

She went to her kitchen and opened the refrigerator and looked over the small assortment of food in there. She grabbed an apple and the remaining piece of cheddar cheese. She went to the bedroom and looked around sadly at the scene it presented. She turned off the light and made the bed. Painful memories of despair tried to flood her mind but she simply turned around and headed back to the kitchen.

She sat at the tiny kitchen table and plugged the phone cord back into the wall jack. She looked through her purse and found Carol's cell phone number.

"Hi Carol?"

"Catherine?"

"Yes, it's me. Guess what? I'm home."

"Oh that's wonderful. How does it feel to be back home?"

"I'm shocked at how dark and dreary my home is. I guess I just got used to it being this way. There's nothing to remind me of Christmas here. I'm looking forward to coming to your party. What do you need me to bring?"

"Nothing really. Just bring yourself and come celebrate with us."

"Thank you Carol. I was wondering what is showing in the calendar house today?"

"It's a Christmas tree. It's not too fancy but it's beautiful nevertheless. It looks like it is in a living room or even a family room."

"That's interesting. I was wondering about the wreath from yesterday. When I came home today I noticed a very similar wreath on my neighbor's door. Maybe these new images are to help me get involved in the world around me. I was even considering knocking on my neighbor's door and introducing myself to see who the neighbor might be but I'm scared at the thought of doing anything like that. What do you think?"

"Well, that's an interesting possibility. It wouldn't hurt to try it out. Maybe you can go buy a poinsettia plant or something like that and give it to your neighbor so if it doesn't pan out you can quickly leave after you hand the gift over."

"That's a good idea but still I feel scared."

"Just do it Catherine and then come over to my house. It'll be wonderful!"

After getting directions to the party and a little more encouragement from Carol, she hung up the phone and resolved to make the attempt. She went shopping and bought a pretty poinsettia plant, a new outfit and a cheese ball for the party.

Nervously she approached the house across the street. Her hands shook as she rang the doorbell. She noticed the beautiful wreath up close. It had red bells and pinecones and what had looked like fruit across the street, now up close appeared to be colorful fabric flowers. Catherine didn't know what to think of it. After a few minutes the door slowly opened and a white haired lady with thick glasses appeared at the door.

"Hello. I'm your neighbor Catherine Daley and I wanted to meet you," Catherine said nervously. The little lady smiled.

"Well, come on in!" She declared brightly.

Soon Catherine found herself inside the tiny living room heavily adorned with Christmas decorations and porcelain figures. The room smelled like perfume and old furniture.

"It's so wonderful to have some company. I don't get out much anymore. I can't see well. Oh by the way my name is Wilma Madison."

"Hello Wilma, it's nice to meet you. This plant is for you."

"Isn't it just beautiful? Thank you so much for you kindness. Please won't you sit down? I can make you a cup of tea and I have a tin of butter cookies we can share."

"That would be wonderful. Thank you."

Catherine proceeded to spend several hours with this sweet woman becoming well acquainted with her history and learned all about her deceased husband, children and grandchildren. Catherine could tell that she was quite lonely. Wilma mentioned a number of times how she wished her family lived closer and that only one of her daughters made much attempt to visit often. One son had invited her to come spend Christmas at his home and she was still deciding about it. She did not like to travel.

Catherine didn't share too much but mostly listened to this witty and kind woman who yearned daily for company. Her heart felt very light and happy when she left Wilma's home and she promised to visit her again soon. Excitedly she went back home and got dressed up, curled her hair and found some old makeup for her aging face. She looked glamorous for the first time in many years. She showed up a few minutes early at Carol's home. Carol was amazed at Catherine's transformation.

"Oh Catherine, you look beautiful! Welcome to my home and come meet my family."

She put her arm around Catherine and began introducing her to everyone present. It was a joyous evening for her and she felt truly welcomed by Carol, her friends and family. Carol's husband John was completely surprised when he met Catherine. Carol had described her appearance quite differently. Now Catherine seemed to glow with beauty. She was so excited to share with Carol the experience she had meeting her neighbor Wilma and how the simple act of reaching out to her neighbor was able to bring such joy into her life. Carol congratulated her for her accomplishment and then gave her the bag with the Christmas calendar house in it.

"What a blessing this is to my life and to think that just a week ago I was calling it a curse!"

The image in the twentieth window was indeed beautiful and revealed a simply decorated Christmas tree. It looked just perfect in the quaint living room setting.

"The tree is very pretty but what on earth could it mean? The wreath on Wilma's door was kind of similar but it wasn't the same as the one in the calendar house. I don't think we are any closer to solving this mystery but it sure felt great today at Wilma's trying to find out."

"I'm just glad you did that. You made someone's life better today. It made you feel happy, didn't it?"

"It sure did. I think I might be on the right path. At least it's making my life better too."

Carol just nodded her head. Catherine slipped the unique wooden house back into the bag as she and Carol rejoined the wonderful Christmas celebration that was full of all that is special about the holiday season: beautiful decorations, delicious food, joyful music, warm friendship and brotherly love.

# *December 21ˢᵗ*

Catherine woke up thinking about Christmas trees. She had wonderful dreams during the night about parties and joyous Christmas celebrations. It had been a long time since she felt so wonderful and refreshed after a night of sleep. It seemed as though the insomnia she suffered from for years was entirely related to her depression and now it just seemed like a bad dream that was over with as well. She thought about the party the previous evening. She had come home late from it, as the party seemed to want to go on forever. She had been offered some alcohol at the party but refused to indulge. She didn't like the effects of alcohol and was uncertain how it might react with the medication she was currently taking. She wondered if everyone else who had been at the party felt so good this morning and then smiled.

Her thoughts turned to some precious memories about Christmas trees. Her family each year would travel to the mountains in search of the perfect fresh Christmas tree to bring back home. She remembered hiking through the forests searching for the right one. It became one of those cherished family traditions that the children looked forward to each year. Catherine enjoyed everything except the deep snow they encountered every other year or so. The best part was snuggling together in the car afterwards enjoying cookies and hot chocolate before heading home. The wonderful scent of a fresh cut fir tree filled the house for days.

She considered getting a Christmas tree of her own but realized she really didn't need one seeing how she would be making plane reservations in a little while to go back home to see her family. However the desire to get a tree and decorate it remained strong. She then thought that perhaps she could get a Christmas tree and decorate it for a family in town that perhaps didn't have a tree at all because they couldn't afford one.

At this point Catherine had no idea how to go about doing this so she called Carol for guidance once again. Carol suggested several charitable organizations to call. She was once again delighted to discover Catherine trying to be charitable and reach out in kindness to others. She had made sure that Catherine had taken the calendar house home the previous evening and now was curious about what it showed today. Catherine had been thinking so hard about Christmas trees that she had forgotten to look at the calendar house today. She put the phone down and went over to the bag in the darkened living room. Now the brightly lit up windows glowed in the darkness, which entirely excited Catherine when she glanced at it again. In the twenty first window there was an adorable sleigh just filled with presents wrapped in all sorts of beautiful Christmas paper. The sleigh appeared to be a decoration in someone's home. It was a delightful scene. Catherine went over and picked up the phone.

"The window shows a really cute sleigh and it's all full of wrapped Christmas presents. From what I can tell it looks to be a decoration in someone's home and is not the size of a real sleigh but it's quite charming. You should see it."

"I can't wait to see it. It seems to me like everything is related together somehow like the presents should go with the Christmas tree."

"Maybe it is just another reminder for me to do some gift giving, which is many years overdue."

"You're probably right. Look how much you're enjoying Christmas now. Wait until you start giving gifts. That's when we really begin to feel the Spirit of Christmas especially when we give of ourselves. Did you make plane reservations yet?"

"Not yet. I've got plenty to do today. Thanks for your help. Have a wonderful day with your family. Thanks so much for inviting me to you party. I had a great time. It was so fun."

"I'm so glad you came. That was a fun party. You did very well and everyone enjoyed having you there. No one would have believed that you were just released from a mental hospital."

"Did you tell anyone?"

"No, of course not. The only person who knew besides me was John and he wouldn't go say anything like that to anyone. He's pretty reserved. Catherine, have a wonderful day and have fun shopping."

After she hung up with Carol, she immediately called Dr. Thomas and left a message to have him call her so she could share some of the joy she was experiencing since leaving the hospital. She called her sister after that but she wasn't there. Catherine left a message about trying to find out when Tina was flying home so they might be able to coordinate flights. She asked Tina to call her back soon. She called her mother and let her know that she would be coming home for Christmas and she was trying to coordinate her travel plans with Tina. Catherine's mother was very pleased when she heard the good news. She was also delighted to hear Catherine share some of the joy she was having trying to celebrate Christmas again. Catherine could sense her mother's happiness that only added to own happiness as she said goodbye and hung up the phone.

Catherine called the places Carol had suggested and found out there was a number of families in need of her kindness. She felt overwhelmed when she discovered so many families were suffering. She wanted to help them all but started to get discouraged at the prospect of trying to help them. She thought to call Carol but just then Dr. Thomas called her back.

"Hello Catherine? So how did you do yesterday?"

"Hi Dr. Thomas. I did really well. The party was great. I haven't had that much fun in years. I am starting to feel really different about Christmas. I want to celebrate it again."

"That is just marvelous. Have you felt discouraged or down at all?"

"As a matter of fact I was just starting to feel discouraged when you called."

"What are you feeling discouraged about?"

"There are so many people that need help to have a nice Christmas. I mean they don't even have gifts or a Christmas tree or money to get a nice meal. I want to help but how can I do any good when there are so many?"

Dr. Thomas could sense Catherine's frustration in her voice. He was quite pleased to hear that her discouragement centered on trying to be benevolent. He had encouraged Catherine to go serve in the community for a long time but with no avail. He had discovered how much helping others seems to diminish the severity of a person's own problems. He had his wife to thank for teaching him this principle. Now he welcomed such opportunities and the happiness it brought.

"Well you are right about there being many people in need, especially this time of year. You can't possibly help them all but you can do something for a few. That's all you can ask of yourself. Decide what you want to accomplish and then ask yourself how you want to go about it."

"I called three charitable organizations and they all mentioned they had a lot of families who could use a Christmas tree, food and some gifts. That's what I want to do."

"Well, have each charity select one family for you and that will make three families to help. That is a lot. Do you think you can do that much? It seems a bit overwhelming for just one person to try to do and expensive too. Do you have the resources?"

"I have money, time and the desire. I hope I can do three families. I'll do one and see how it goes. Thank you so much for your advice. I took a poinsettia plant over to a neighbor yesterday and I had a wonderful time getting to know the woman named Wilma. She was quite lonely and seemed to enjoy my company."

"You did have a very good day yesterday, didn't you? I am so proud of you Catherine. Keep this marvelous progress up and have a fun time helping others today."

She thanked the good doctor and hung up, but first promising him that she would continue to update him on how things were going. Catherine called the first charity back and requested they select one name. She wrote down the information about the family, how many and what they needed. Soon she was ready to go shopping. She ventured in a number of stores having the time of her life. It reminded her of Ebenezer Scrooge on Christmas morning when he excitedly went Christmas shopping after his nightlong visits from the ghosts of Christmas past, present and future. She loved buying several dolls, games and other toys for the children in the family. However, it was bringing back the bittersweet memories of shopping for her three children many years ago. She struggled a bit and at one point had to call Carol for a dash of encouragement to keep going. Carol was glad to oblige and reminded her of the miracles of the calendar house that had helped Catherine deal with her loss and that her children were probably rejoicing at her efforts to help other children. This really helped lift her heart and gave her some strength to persevere joyfully. She selected some clothing and other items for the family. She bought food for a Christmas feast and few extra staples.

Finally she ventured into the Christmas section of the department store and bought some beautiful but simple Christmas tree ornaments, lights and garland, similar to the kind she saw on the tree in the twentieth window. She stopped at a tree lot and purchased a medium sized fresh tree and stand. She had the tree tied to the roof of her car just like her husband did with the fresh tree cut during their yearly adventure to the woods. She went home and prepared to wrap all the gifts up. First she spruced up her home a little and attempted to decorate it. She bought several Christmas decorations for her home to help brighten up her home a bit. She set up a small-decorated artificial tree on top of her television; put a pretty wreath on her door and a floral centerpiece with a candle on her kitchen table. She turned on the radio and found some likeable holiday music. Suddenly her little home didn't seem quite so dreary anymore. This really helped lighten her heart as she set about wrapping the pile of gifts she purchased. A special warmth seemed to envelop Catherine as she lovingly wrapped each gift, imagining how the child might react and play with it. She packed up the gifts and added a few extra items she found around her home to the box. She drove over to the home. It was in a neighborhood that was not too far from her part of town.

The house looked smaller than her home. She felt nervous about approaching the family so she decided to pull up the driveway and simply start unloading the boxes and tree on the porch as quietly as possible. No one seemed to take notice and she was almost finished when a small girl about five years old came out of the house and saw her. She got a big grin on her face, went over and hugged Catherine tightly around the waist and then ran to tell her family inside. Soon the entire family that consisted of the parents and four children all pretty young came out to see what was going on. Not much was said except several expressions of simple but embarrassed gratitude. Catherine just smiled back and said Merry Christmas to the family as she quickly got into the car and drove away. The family waved to her as she left.

She sang Christmas carols joyfully as she went home. Catherine hadn't sung anything for many years. It felt good to sing again along to the merry tunes that played in her head that she had heard earlier in the day when she was wrapping gifts. She checked her answering machine for messages when she got home and was glad to hear the message from her sister Tina. She was flying out of Seattle on December 22 after she got off work. She would be connecting in Chicago and then flying onto Boston. From there she would rent a car and drive up to New Hampshire.

Catherine called a travel agent and asked if there were any flights out of Denver that would match up with Tina's to Chicago and then on to Boston. The travel agent said she would check then call her back and let her know. In the meantime Catherine thought about the experience of getting the gifts, food and tree for this humble little family. It was quite unlike anything she had ever experienced before. She wanted to do it again and then looked at the clock to see if she had enough time remaining. It was pretty late in the afternoon so she decided that she would pursue it again tomorrow. Now she wanted to go get gifts for friends and family and fill up a sleigh like the sleigh in the twenty first window, just full of beautifully wrapped gifts to give to everyone she knew and pretend to be Santa Claus for a while.

# *December 22nd*

    Catherine had spent the remainder of the previous evening shopping. She stopped for a quick bite to eat at the mall food court and simply enjoyed the atmosphere the busy last minute shoppers created. It was fun to be around people again, observing them and seeing how they interacted with each other. She especially enjoyed watching the families as it reminded her of the precious little family she had the opportunity to help.

    Her arms were full of bags with gifts for her parents and sister, Carol, Dr. Thomas, Wilma, Alice, Maurice and even Frank Barton. She went home and enjoyed wrapping everything while she watched her old favorite Christmas movie, "It's a Wonderful Life" that was on television. This was the first Christmas movie she had watched in a very long time. She hadn't seen the movie in years and now saw it in a different light. She somehow felt very connected to George Bailey at the end of the movie when he realized his life was worthwhile after all. Catherine recognized the special advent calendar house that had revolutionized her life in a short time had completely changed how she felt about her life and that it was going to be wonderful again. George needed to experience what Bedford Falls could have been like without him ever being born to help him truly see what he really had. Despite the fact that our lives are sometimes full of many obstacles, heartaches and disappointments, life is an amazing gift from God and shouldn't be thrown away.

Before she went to bed she admired the shining calendar house once more, which was by far the most beautiful Christmas decoration she possessed. She looked once again at the darling sleigh full of gifts in the 21$^{st}$ window and then glanced at the pile of her own brightly wrapped presents with shiny bows and felt merry inside as she looked forward to delivering some of the gifts the next day.

She awoke to the telephone ringing. She looked at her watch and it was nine in the morning already. Catherine had enjoyed another wonderful night of sleep and she was delighted. She answered the phone call and it was the travel agent calling her back. She had left a message on the machine the previous afternoon that Catherine had managed to overlook with all of her shopping trips and then spending the entire evening in her living room, wrapping and watching the Christmas movie on television. The travel agent was unable to find a good match with Tina's travel itinerary because of the high volume of holiday travelers and all of the possible flights were completely booked. Catherine felt disappointed she wouldn't be able to join Tina at the same time for this special homecoming. She tried not to get discouraged at this point and told the travel agent to do her best at finding travel arrangements back to New Hampshire leaving no later than tomorrow the twenty third.

Catherine hurriedly got ready for the day, anxious to make her deliveries and leave enough time to help another family in need today. She picked up the Calendar house that she had left in the living room and glanced at the twenty-second window. It showed a lovely upright piano that featured a book of favorite Christmas hymns and a beautiful display of pine branches, poinsettias and little white baby's breath flowers. It seemed to remind Catherine of the piano she once had in her own living room. Her daughter Susie was just starting to get a handle on playing the piano when the accident occurred. She was learning to play "Joy to the World" and "Jingle Bells" for her piano teacher and had recently performed at her first piano recital. Catherine pondered on this memory and recalled the sound of Susie carefully playing both songs and feeling so proud about her daughter's musical accomplishment.

She thought about music now and how she didn't seem to listen to it much anymore. On the way to work Catherine often tuned in to talk show radio even though she would find much of the conversations tiresome. It provided a small connection to what was happening in the real world and she could easily shut it off if she found it too much for her ears. Catherine wondered if there was any opportunity to perhaps attend a Christmas music concert before she left town. She looked at the paper while she ate her breakfast of oatmeal and toast. There was to be a concert that evening located at a church downtown. The advertisement said it would be hosting a variety of singers and musicians from around the area and promised to provide a nice variety of holiday music and some beloved hymns. She had a busy day to look forward to and now a nice community event to attend. Certainly the concert would satisfy her sudden desire to hear music again, especially Christmas music.

The thought occurred to her to call Dr. Thomas on his cell phone before she got too busy and let him know she had another good day yesterday and that the tree and gift giving to the family had gone very well and she wanted to do it again. He was very pleased when she called.

"Good morning, Catherine. From the sound of your voice, you seem to be doing well today. How did yesterday go?"

"It was so great. Those little faces with big eyes full of joy made it all worthwhile. Thank you again for your advice. I am going to attempt to do another family today. I still don't have my plane reservations but I plan on leaving tomorrow. Are you going to be at your office today?"

"I plan on being there this morning but I have plans with my wife for the afternoon. Why do you ask?"

"I just wanted to see you again before I go away," Catherine hesitated to say anything about the gift she bought him and decided to completely surprise him later.

"That would be nice. I think the ladies in the office would like to see you again. I've been telling them all about your remarkable recovery and they are very excited for you."

"It seems they have only seen me at my worst. I'll look forward to seeing them again and you too."

"I am so glad everything went well yesterday. I'll see you later."

She called Carol to tell her she would be by in a little while and she would bring the Calendar house by too so she could see it.

"What does it show today?"

"A beautiful piano. It looks like it is in a living room or den like the Christmas tree and sleigh were. It reminded me of the piano we used to have in our home long ago. Susie was taking lessons at the time and she just starting to get pretty good at playing the piano when the accident happened," Catherine sighed, "I wonder if she was still here what she would sound like now at the piano."

"She probably would sound just divine."

"Oh Carol. It's so hard to be without my wonderful children. Wrapping all of the gifts for those children yesterday only reminded me of buying and wrapping gifts for Susie, Jimmy and Jenny. I'm enjoying all of this but it is still so painful for me."

"I know. Christmas brings out the strongest and sweetest memories in us. We miss our loved the ones the most this time of year. Remembering them is a way to make them present in your life. When you pushed all memories of them out of your life all those years it just made your life hollow. Now your life can be rich and full all the while not shunning those precious memories of your family. Remember the pain you feel now will be turned to joy one day when you are reunited with them in heaven. In the meantime, you have much to offer. You have a wonderful heart. You are intelligent and beautiful. There is so much for you to look forward to."

"I hope you are right that I will see them again."

"Of course you will. What does your heart tell you?"

Catherine thought for a moment and felt very peaceful. Her eyes became wet. She thought quietly about seeing and hearing her husband James in her dream and how real he seemed to her. That was something to hold on to. Jenny was as sweet and lovely as ever when she dreamed about her too. When she saw Jimmy's face in the window, he looked so troubled. Perhaps it was his concern for her wellbeing that saddened him. She imagined him smiling now because her life was immensely happier. The only one she hadn't seen in her dreams was Susie but this morning's memory of her playing lovely Christmas tunes was a strong reminder of this precious daughter. Her heart was feeling much hope and faith and she would hold on dearly to that to get her through the rough patches.

"My heart tells me that they are not far from me. The calendar house and my realistic dreams tell me heaven is close. I believe they are there waiting for me."

"Hold that hope close and it will get you through anything life has to throw at you. Keep striving to help those around you and you will be happy no matter what challenges you are facing."

"Dr. Thomas has been trying to tell me that for years. He says it is good therapy for the mind and the heart."

"He's absolutely correct. Wouldn't you agree with that after what you've done the past few days?"

"Absolutely. Thanks Carol for your advice. I'll see you in a little while."

While Catherine was preparing to leave to deliver the presents, the travel agent called back with her travel arrangements.

She would be leaving Denver at 10:30 in the morning changing planes in Chicago and flying onto Boston in the afternoon. A rental car was reserved for her to drive up to New Hampshire. Catherine thanked her and said she would be by later to pick up the tickets.

She called her mother to tell her the good news.

"Hello, Mom?"

"Hi Catherine! It's so good to hear from you. Are you going to come home for Christmas?"

"Yes! I'm coming home tomorrow. I just got off the phone with my travel agent. And I'll be driving up from Boston about 4:00 PM Eastern Time."

"Oh, that's just wonderful. Tina will be here this evening. She was quite apologetic when she called. I'm just glad she's okay. I can't wait to see you both."

"Mom, you are so kind and so forgiving. I can't wait to see you, dad and Tina. I hope the weather is going to cooperate."

"There is a snow storm due in on Christmas Eve so hopefully it won't affect your trip."

Catherine shared a little with her mom about getting out of the hospital and doing some out of the ordinary things to celebrate Christmas this year. Catherine's mom was delighted to hear of her success and told Catherine to bring the calendar house back to New Hampshire so she could see it.

After the phone call ended, she headed over to Dr. Thomas's office first and gave him his gift. He was surprised by the kind gesture. She had selected a beautiful table fountain for him. Catherine remembered him previously mentioning to her that he found fountains soothing and that perhaps he should one day get one for the office. Dr. Thomas opened the gift and found the fountain very much to his liking. He thanked her graciously and wished her all the success and happiness as she returned home to her family. She thanked him for all of his support and therapy and wished him a merry Christmas. The women in the office each gave Catherine a big hug before she left and enthusiastically told her how wonderful she looked and how they were so happy for her success. This was a marvelous experience for Catherine.

Next she headed over to the hospital to find Maurice who she hoped would be found delivering lunch to the patients. She felt strange entering the hospital again but relieved she could leave as soon as she wanted. She heard his whistling and waited for him to come back into the hallway after delivering lunch to the patient in the room.

"Well hello Miss Catherine! What are you doing here?"

"I came to say goodbye and to give you this," Catherine handed him the wrapped gift.

"Why you didn't have to do that. That was so kind of you. Thank you."

"I just wanted to let you know how much help you were to me here in this hospital. You helped get through some very dark days. Your gift is a reminder of the sunlight and happiness you give to others each day."

Maurice took the gift and opened it. He beheld a beautiful crystal cube with a sun etched inside and a rotating pedestal to put it on with a light at the bottom. It was a simple but beautiful gift and Maurice loved it. He gave Catherine a big hug and wished her a blessed Christmas as she left. She returned the greeting as she walked down the hall, wiping away the tears. She enjoyed giving gifts to people. She smiled and waved to the people she recognized there as she left.

She stopped at Carol's house and didn't want to stay too long as she could see Carol was busy playing with her grandson and baking cookies. She handed the bag with the calendar house and Carol took it to her bedroom. Catherine followed and the two women discussed the beautiful sleigh with gifts and the piano. Carol was trying to piece together the puzzle the scenes presented and Catherine was busy trying to share with Carol the joy she experienced giving gifts to Dr. Thomas and Maurice. Catherine hadn't been dwelling on the mystery meaning of the scenes in windows since the nineteenth as she was satisfied they were just there to help her reconnect with the world. Carol agreed that was probably the reason but part of her still wondered and hoped that somehow the mystery would be completely solved by the twenty fourth. Catherine pulled out the wrapped present for Carol from the bag. She opened the box. It was a beautiful sculpture of two women, one giving flowers to the other. At the bottom was a message that said, "Friendship is a Priceless Gift". Carol's eyes moistened when she beheld the lovely gift and the simple but true message it declared.

"Thank you for this. It's just beautiful. What a great reminder of our special friendship,"

"How can I thank you enough?"

"The way you're living your life now is how. I have a gift for you too."

She went to her closet and grabbed the box on the floor.

"We have to hide the presents from my grandson or he opens them all. Here, open this."

Catherine chuckled at that. She opened the box and inside she found a beautiful nativity set and a smaller box that contained a necklace with a heart pendant. She thanked Carol for both. She loved them and would cherish the gifts. Carol mentioned that she got the nativity set because she probably didn't own one or much jewelry either and reminded Catherine of the importance of trusting her heart to God. Catherine smiled and then told Carol her travel plans for the next day and the women realized this would probably be the last time together for a while. Catherine promised she would call and let her know how things turned out back east. It was hard to say goodbye. The women gave each other a big hug and wished each other a Merry Christmas.

She entered the office of Precise Accounting Services with some fear. It was time to face Frank Barton again. Before she did, she found Alice and handed her a gift.

"Thank you for your kindness, Alice. Have a Merry Christmas."

Alice looked up surprised at Catherine and then gave her a big smile.

"Hello Catherine! Thank you for the gift. You didn't have to do that. How kind you are. What a pleasant surprise to see you again. How are you doing?"

"I'm doing so much better."

"I can tell. That's so wonderful. When are you coming back to work?"

"I'm not."

"Oh that's too bad. What are you going to do?"

"I'm flying home tomorrow to see my family who I haven't seen in years and after that, I am not sure what I am going to do. I'm taking it a day at a time right now. I just need to do something different with my life."

"I understand. Well, best of luck to you and I hope you have a wonderful Christmas with your family."

"Thanks, I hope you do too.  Merry Christmas Alice."

"Merry Christmas to you too, Catherine."

Catherine headed to Frank Barton's office and started to get a nervous feeling in her stomach.  She was about to leave when she sat down and collected her thoughts and did her best to face her fears.

"Hello Mr. Barton."

Frank looked up at her with complete surprise.

"Catherine!  How are you doing?"

"I'm doing much better.  I just wanted to let you know that I am not going to return to work here anymore."

"Oh, why is that?"

"Well, I have made quite a recovery since you last saw me and I am ready to move on and do something different with my life.  I wanted to thank you for allowing me to work here for all these years.  Have a Merry Christmas and goodbye."  She handed him the gift of a small desk clock and left the office.  He was too shocked to speak.  She quickly left the building with her heart pounding and finished up her errands before heading back home. She stopped by to see Wilma again.  She gave her a porcelain snowman that had an adorable face that looked happy.  Catherine said it made her happy to meet and visit with Wilma.  She apologized for not coming by to meet her sooner.   Wilma had decided to go stay with her son for Christmas so Catherine was relieved she wouldn't be by herself for the holiday.

Catherine quickly packed her bag and got ready for her trip the next morning. She was so excited. It was getting late in the afternoon but she made the effort to get another family name and address and hurried to the store to purchase the needed items. She felt a bit stronger than yesterday doing the shopping for the three children on the list. Perhaps she was working through her pain as her faith and hope grew. She hurriedly got the remaining items and had the presents gift-wrapped as she went to purchase some food and tree decorations. She picked up a tree on the way to the little home that was not too far from the other home. Once again she quietly unloaded the items and tree. This time, no one noticed and she drove away. She pictured in her mind, the surprise and delight in the children's faces when they realized a secret Santa had just visited them.

Catherine drove over to her favorite restaurant and enjoyed the meal. She felt so good. It was hard to contain her joy. The owner of the restaurant came over and remarked how wonderful she looked and inquired how she was doing. Normally she was known as the customer who kept to herself. Catherine enjoyed speaking with the owner and learning his name. She shared a little about herself and what had been happening. He told her that dinner was on the house to help her celebrate her success. This seemed to make the wonderful day even better.

The concert was just what she was anticipating. She loved hearing the carols performed by a variety of talented singers accompanied by a full orchestra. She decided she loved music and it was something she truly missed in her life. It was right then that she resolved to get a handsome piano, just like the one she saw in the calendar window, take lessons and learn to play beautiful music just like her daughter Susie. She left the concert full of excitement, turned on the radio to enjoy more carols and drove through the streets admiring the colorful display of Christmas lights on the many homes in the delightful Colorado town. It was a lovely ending to a memorable day.

# *December 23rd*

Catherine woke up to the wonderful sound of a Christmas carol playing in her head. Right now "Joy to the World" was resonating in her head almost as brilliantly as she heard being played the previous evening at the concert. Today she would see her parents and sister again after many years. How many years exactly she couldn't recall off hand so she sat up and thought about it for a few minutes. She reflected again on how she had reacted to the insults and criticisms during a time of extreme stress and heartache. Her decision to up and move to the west was rash and made very quickly. Now in perspective most of the blame for the fights rested mostly on Catherine. She seemed to recall with intense detail the conversations with both her mother and sister. Catherine realized her guilt had overshadowed everything. The guilt for all of what happened was now gone. The anger had melted away too. It was a great miracle. A long chapter in her book of life was now closed. She was glad and grateful a new one had begun with her beloved family. Christmas is all about family and she was delighted to be able to spend Christmas once again with them.

She had about an hour drive to the Denver airport ahead of her not including the possibility of delays from extra holiday traffic and winter weather so she hurried to get ready. She spent a few extra minutes putting on makeup, curling her hair and selecting her best outfit for traveling so she would look her best when she saw her family again. She found a medium blue blazer with a white collared blouse and navy slacks. She added a pretty holiday pin of a wreath on the blazer. She finished loading the car and was ready to leave when she realized she had not remembered the Christmas calendar house. She grabbed the cloth bag with the calendar house in it. She pulled it out and looked at the twenty-third window and it showed a nativity scene not too unlike the beautiful one Carol had given her the previous day. She went to her bedroom and carefully examined the nativity set again that she had set up on her dresser. It was similar but not identical to the one in the window. She sat and pondered the pieces of the set.

It had been years since she contemplated the Christmas story. Catherine had made considerable progress in her faith since all these miracles began occurring to her. She now had a sweet assurance of the reality of heaven and of heavenly help. She looked carefully at the infant Jesus in the manger. It was easy in this day and age to celebrate Christmas with all the tremendous barrage of commercialism, bright lights and tinsel without considering the very reason for the existence of the holiday in the first place. Now the reality of His miraculous birth seemed to overwhelm her thoughts. Catherine again felt the peaceful feeling that enveloped her yesterday when she considered her family and being reunited with them again and now the feeling reassured her that this infant, who was born in the most humble of circumstances, was the Son of God.

She gently lifted up the figurine of Mary to examine her sweet face and thought for a moment what it might have been like to be the mother of one so great as the Son of God, and one that would have to see him later suffer and die on the cross. She looked lovingly at the rest of the figures of the nativity and felt grateful for an increase in her understanding of the love of God that he was willing to send his Son to earth to be our Lord and Savior. She looked forward to sharing these feelings with her mother who had always shared with Catherine her faith in God. It had sustained Catherine for a long time until the tragedy of the accident shattered that fragile faith. Now the feelings of faith in God were stirring in her heart and she knew this of herself. It was another miracle.

Catherine suddenly felt the urgency of leaving for the airport on time so she grabbed a couple good paperback novels she had purchased to read to make the day of travel go by faster that were on her bedside table. She put the calendar house in the bag along with the novels and left the house. The sky looked heavy with clouds and the winds were beginning to increase. She hoped she would be able to fly out of Denver before the snowstorm arrived.

She hadn't done much traveling since first moving to Colorado so she enjoyed seeing the scenery of the Rockies covered with snow and the clouds from the approaching storm. She had chosen to move to Colorado because it was the first place she found a job and it was a sizeable distance away from New England.

She didn't have a difficult time finding the airport and long-term parking. Soon she was checking in her bags and getting her boarding pass. Catherine still had forty-five minutes until they started boarding her plane. She eagerly sat down and started reading her novel. She made sure of her bag that contained the precious advent calendar house and her purse from time to time. The interesting novel helped divert her attention and the time passed quickly.

Catherine really didn't enjoy flying very much. She had only flown twice before in her life. The first time was when she was first in college and the second time was with James when they were celebrating their fifth wedding anniversary. He had surprised her with a trip to Florida for a few days. Her parents had watched Susie and little Jimmy. It was a fun trip but the flight had been bumpy and she felt nervous and her stomach was upset for most of the time they were in the air. She sat next to the window, tried to relax after buckling her seat belt and listened to the instructions being given by the flight attendant. The flight was very crowded. She smiled at the woman passenger sitting next to her but no conversation occurred between them. She picked up the novel and tried her best on focus on it while the jet took off powerfully. Fortunately the flight was fairly smooth for most of the trip to Chicago. When the plane landed at O'Hare Airport, she waited patiently as many of the passengers got off in a hurry. She still had an hour to get to her next plane before it departed to Boston.

She grabbed a sandwich and a soda at a deli and continued to read her book. The airport bustled with travelers anxious to get home to celebrate the holiday with their loved ones. She headed over to the departure gate and checked in. It was a short wait until she was once again seated in the airplane, this time in the middle seat. She felt crowded. She had a woman at her left that looked like a businesswoman. A man smiled at her when he sat down in the seat next to hers. He was friendly she could tell. She hesitated talking to him because she wanted to continue reading her book that was just starting to get really intense. She was relieved when he pulled out a book as well. She read for quite a while. Catherine started to feel sleepy. She dozed off for about twenty minutes and woke up feeling nervous. She doubled checked her purse and bag that contained the calendar house that were under the seat in front of her.

The gentlemen next to her watched her as she opened the bag and looked inside. What he saw made him very curious. After Catherine resumed reading her book he decided he would try to make conversation with her.

"What are you reading there?"

Catherine looked up for a moment, said nothing but showed him the cover of her book.

"Is it a good book?"

She nodded, smiling.

"I can't seem to get into the book I brought. It is a real slow starter. Oh, by the way, my name is Doug Anderson. What is your name?"

"Catherine Daley."

"It's nice to meet you."

Doug was struggling to keep the conversation going without asking too many more questions. Catherine definitely didn't seem interested in talking to him. His curiosity about the object in the bag kept him persisting.

"I'm heading back home to Concord, New Hampshire. How about you?"

"I'm going back to see family not far from there myself."

"Oh really? What part?"

"A bit north of there, off I-93 a little ways," Catherine wanted to remain vague to this complete stranger with the gentle smile.

"Where are you from?"

"Colorado"

"Beautiful place I hear."

"Yes it is."

Doug was getting really impatient and found himself just blurting out, "I saw what was in your bag down there. It looked really interesting and I was wondering if you would be willing to show it to me."

This completely surprised Catherine. She wanted to refuse him being annoyed by his abruptness and nosiness. Then the thought occurred to her that perhaps he was seeing the calendar house like it truly was and not just a piece of wood. She hesitated and then agreed. She grabbed the bag and handed it to him. He looked inside and gasped.

"It's beautiful. What is it?"

"So you see a house full of little lit up windows?"

"Yes."

"Oh my goodness."

"What? You still haven't told me what it is. I have never seen anything quite like it."

Catherine's heart pounded, not sure how to answer him.

"It's an advent calendar. See, there are twenty-four windows and all but the last one for tomorrow is lit up. Each one has a scene about Christmas."

"Wow. That's amazing. Where did you get this?"

"I'm not sure. It showed up on my doorstep on December 1st. I have no idea where it came from or how it works."

Doug handed it back to her, shaking his head in amazement. She put it back under the seat.

Catherine wasn't sure what to say next to this man. They both sat silently for a few minutes. She was hoping that he wouldn't pry any more into her personal life and ask her more questions. He in turn didn't know what to ask next but his curiosity about the advent calendar remained high. A flight attendant who asked what they wanted for a beverage interrupted the awkward moment. She decided to avoid him by trying to read more of her novel and sip her drink. She read for quite a while again and he tried to read his novel too. The plane was beginning its slow decent into Boston. Catherine started to feel excited and nervous at the same time. She didn't know what to think about this gentleman next to her that could see the calendar house as clearly as she could. What could it possibly mean? She wanted desperately to call Carol and ask her what she thought about it all.

After the plane landed, Doug turned to her once more and asked if he could see the advent calendar one last time. She agreed he could after they got off the plane since there were so many people hovering around them, waiting to get off the plane. He followed her into the terminal. She handed him the bag again. He took it out and studied it in amazement for a few minutes.

"Wow, the scenes in the last few windows remind me of my own home. That's pretty cool. Well, I'd love to hear the whole story about how you got this but I know you are in a hurry to get home to your family. I need to get home to my family too. Here's my phone number if you feel like calling me some time to talk about this. It was a pleasure meeting you Catherine."

"It was nice to meet you too. You are only the third person that has seen this special advent calendar house. I was glad to show it to you too. Have a wonderful Christmas."

Doug stuck out his hand and she shook it. It felt warm and familiar and for a moment took her back in time to another warm hand pulling her up from the ice. She smiled at him. He waved at her as he walked down the concourse.

She used the ladies room to freshen up and headed to get her luggage and secure the rental car. She thought about Doug Anderson on and off on her way to New Hampshire. She was still unable to determine what it all possibly meant. It was well after dark by the time she got to her parents' home.

She felt nervous and excited as she rang the doorbell. Her mother answered the door and embraced Catherine for a long while. It felt so good. She came into the house and Tina excitedly rushed over to her and gave her big sister a huge hug. Catherine went over to her dad who was sitting down in his armchair and reached down and kissed him on the cheek. He stood up and gave his daughter a big hug. Nothing was said for a minute. Everyone felt too joyful for words.

# December 24th

The family had sat up until late in the evening after having dinner together sharing stories and catching up on each other's lives. Catherine's parents and sister were simply amazed by the advent calendar. Catherine's parents enjoyed viewing the first few windows which reminded them of things from Christmases past when the girls were little. They asked Catherine many questions about it and she shared what she had experienced with it and what she thought about it. She kept shaking her head in amazement as she related the different days that had transpired and the memories the calendar house had conjured up. Catherine especially enjoyed getting reacquainted with Tina again. The sisters stayed up talking until late in the night in their old bedroom. It was fun sharing the room again like they used to. It was a great beginning to their holiday together.

Catherine and Tina both woke up late about the same time. They smelled bacon and coffee and ventured downstairs in their bathrobes. Catherine studied the happy but aging faces of her dear parents sitting at the kitchen table. She hugged them both again and told them how much she loved them and how wonderful it was to be home. Both ladies sat down at the table.

"What are your plans today Catherine?" Her mom asked.

"Well, I wanted to go see Peggy Swanson if possible. Every time I see the Christmas tree necklace in that window it reminds me about her."

"That advent calendar house is such an amazing thing, Catherine," her dad mentioned.

"Well, you're the second man that can see it. I met a man on the plane yesterday that could see it as well. Dr. Thomas only saw a piece of wood. I am not sure why. It's all so strange to me. I think the man on the plane wanted to ask me all about it but was afraid to ask. He gave me his phone number. His name is Doug Anderson and he lives in Concord."

"Doug Anderson?" Catherine's mom asked.

"Yes. Do you know him?"

"I know something about him, if he's the same Doug Anderson. I heard that he lost his wife last year to cancer. He's a nice man with four children. That's about all I know of him."

"How do you know all of this?"

"My friend Janette Wilson knows him and told me all about his ordeal. The poor man, I feel sorry for him. I guess she really lingered a long time with brain cancer."

"That's so sad. He didn't say anything about that; just that he had a family he needed to get home to. Speaking of cancer, how are you feeling today, Dad?"

"Not too bad, especially because I have my two beautiful daughter's home and my lovely wife to keep me happy. Come give me another hug." Both ladies obliged him. Tina looked happily at Catherine. She still looked young and fresh faced to Catherine. Her dark brown hair cut short framed her face nicely and her soft brown eyes with long dark eyelashes sparkled with a special glow. She looked more like her mom than ever.

"Do you have all of your shopping done?" Catherine's mom asked.

"It's almost done. I think I might make a trip into town to finish it up after I go see Peggy. Let's get together for dinner later at that wonderful little Italian restaurant we used to go to. Is it still here?"

"Yes. That would be fun. I'll call to see if it is open on Christmas Eve. We should go to dinner early. I also have some shopping to do and I wanted to make a Christmas tree coffeecake for Christmas morning today. How about you Tina?"

"I want to bake cookies just like I used to. I can go shopping with you too mom or stay home with dad," Tina added.

That reminded Catherine about the cookie in the calendar house window.

"Did you make any gingerbread cookies yet?"

"Yes. I did make a batch last week."

"I wonder if it was the same day the gingerbread man appeared in the window. Isn't this just amazing?"

"It really is! Thank goodness for it because look at us now together. This is the miracle that it helped bring about," Tina responded excitedly.

"Yes it is. Speaking of the calendar house, I haven't looked at the twenty-fourth window yet," Catherine went to the living room and picked it up. She stared at the scene and was shocked to see her name on a stocking on a hearth. She ran back to the kitchen to show her family.

"Look at this!" Catherine handed the calendar house to her mother. Tina went over and looked at it with her.

"What does this mean?" Catherine's mom asked. "Your name is on a stocking along with others on a hearth? We don't own any stockings."

Catherine at that moment got a crazy idea to go get the entire family stockings and put their names on them and fill them with presents and goodies and be a secret Santa again. The calendar house had just given her another great idea to help her feel the Spirit of Christmas in a fun and loving way. She was excited to get going to complete this new project before Christmas morning arrived. Her parents and sister would be surprised. She would make herself one just like the one in the window so her family wouldn't know she was the one who made them. Maybe they would think it was a miracle. She laughed to herself at the thought.

She went and called Carol who was very busy but glad to hear from Catherine.

"How was your flight and how are your parents and sister?"

"Both flights were good, not too turbulent. My family is doing well. We had a great time last night getting reacquainted with each other. It was really fun."

"Oh how wonderful. What about the calendar house? What do the last two windows reveal? I'm dying to find out!"

"Yesterday there was scene of a nativity similar to the one you gave me and today, there is a mantle with stockings and one of them has my name on it. What do you think of that? It gave me a great idea to get some stockings for my family and put their names on them and fill them up with gifts and treats secretly. I would do one for me as well so they wouldn't know that I did it for them."

"That's a cute idea. So it seems the mystery we were trying to solve is just like what you said. That all of the things we've seen in the windows since the nineteenth have been reminders of things to do to help you celebrate Christmas with those around you. How did the nativity scene help you?"

"It made me ponder on the real meaning of Christmas and I got some strong peaceful feelings about the infant Jesus being the Son of God and really feeling God's immense love for me and everyone else in sending His son to earth to be our Savior. It was quite amazing. I want to talk to my mom about it."

"What a great gift you've been given Catherine."

"Yes, I know."

Catherine then thought about the interesting fact that both her dad and Doug Anderson could see the calendar house, which proved their theory wrong about men not being able to see it.

"I showed the calendar house to a man on the plane yesterday and he saw it just as plainly as both you and me. My whole family can see it too, including my dad. What do you think about that?"

"Well that's wonderful. It makes me feel saner. Tell me more about this guy you met."

"His name is Doug Anderson and he lives in Concord just south of here. He might be the Doug Anderson my mom told me about this morning who lost his wife last year to cancer. He gave me his phone number to call sometime as he wants to hear more about the calendar house."

"Wow. What did he look like?"

"He was a nice looking man with a gentle smile and a warm handshake."

"He sounds interesting. You should definitely call him."

"What if he's not the same Doug Anderson?"

"Well just tell him about the calendar house and leave it at that."

Catherine proceeded to tell Carol what she wanted to do that day and how she was planning on visiting Peggy Swanson and that she had plenty to do and needed to go. Carol wished her a merry Christmas again and thanked her again for calling.

She called Peggy on the phone and Peggy was so excited to hear from Catherine and to find out that she was in town once again. Catherine apologized to Peggy for her mistreatment and asked for her forgiveness. Peggy reassured her that she had no hard feelings towards Catherine but was so excited to see her again. Catherine got ready for the day as quickly as she could. She enjoyed seeing Tina and her mom working together on making holiday treats in the kitchen before she left.

The predicted snowstorm had arrived and it was snowing hard as Catherine drove over to Peggy's house. It was difficult to see Peggy confined to a wheelchair and Catherine could see a significant reduction in her strength and vitality but her smile was as wonderful as Catherine could remember it. The two ladies spent quite a long time visiting, reminiscing over the good times they had as children growing up together. The friendship seemed to pick up where it was once left and the feelings of closeness resumed. Catherine was so grateful to renew a special bond with this precious person who had been dealing with much loneliness and suffering herself. Catherine had brought the unique calendar house with her to show Peggy. She was able to see and admire the beauty of the house herself too. She noticed the Christmas tree pendant in the 18th window and said that she had worn it just last week. She liked to wear it at least once a year to remind her of Catherine.

Catherine was amazed at the kindness of Peggy and was so grateful to have this opportunity to see her again. The women promised to see each other again after Christmas. Catherine resolved to get Peggy another gift, as she was touched by the way Peggy would wear the pendant simply to remind her about Catherine and to wish her well.

She nervously drove to go shopping in the heavy snowfall. Driving was slow and treacherous and it reminded her of driving in Colorado. She was just grateful that she missed all of this by traveling yesterday. It certainly would be a wonderfully white New England Christmas this year. She was able to get the supplies for her stocking project and the remaining Christmas presents for her family and started driving back home. The wind had picked up and trying to see in the storm proved nearly impossible.

As she drove slowly down the hill towards her parent's house she started to think about Doug Anderson again. She looked over at the calendar house resting on the seat next to her. She recalled his smile, his warm handshake but then she remembered something else he had said when he looked at the house a second time. He said the last few windows reminded him of his own home. Suddenly Catherine heard the terrible sound of tires screeching before the sound of shattering glass and a whirlwind of motion sent her spinning and rolling down the side of the hill. The last thing she remembered was the split second explosion of a white airbag in her face.

Catherine was in a dark quiet place. She was completely unaware of anyone but herself. She couldn't feel any pain. In the distance she saw what looked like an image of a car accident scene but she didn't feel any need to go over there. It didn't matter.

In the distance she could see a light that was very bright. She felt drawn towards that light. She felt herself moving towards the light quickly. It felt lovely and warm the closer she got to it. Suddenly she saw the outline of four people in the light. All at once her family stood before her. They looked beautiful and happy. It was time to be with them again Catherine thought gratefully. Her husband James spoke gently to her.

"It is not time for you to be with us yet. There is a family that needs you. They need your love, Catherine. You must go back."

"What do you mean? James, I can't go back. We are together again! I really hoped I could be with you again. I have missed you all so much. You darling children look so wonderful. Oh how I want to be with you all again!" Catherine longed to embrace them all but something was preventing her.

"We love and miss you so much too. We know you are getting well now. You just needed a little help."

"I know I was very sick. My heart was broken. I was in the very depths of despair. I lived a shallow life at best. I needed a lot of help and it came in the form of a strange advent calendar house that looked very similar to the home we had together once. It reminded me of so many wonderful and important things that I had forgotten about. I saw so many things from my past. It helped me overcome my fears and now I have a wonderful relationship again with my parents and sister. It made me remember how blessed I was to have you all in my life for a time. It helped me to have joy once again in my life."

James smiled and nodded his head as Catherine shared her feelings about the calendar house. She looked lovingly at him.

"We had the calendar house made especially for you Catherine. We hoped it would heal your very special heart, and it has. You must leave us now. You still have work to do and you must return. We will be waiting for you. We love you Catherine."

"I love you all so much! Thank you for caring so much about me. Thank you for the lovely calendar house. I will treasure it always."

Catherine studied tenderly the lovely faces of her children. They radiated love. She yearned to embrace them and talk gently to each one but she felt herself being pulled away from them as quickly as she had move towards them. She saw them in the distance, James was carrying something in his hands as they turned and walked towards the light.

Suddenly Catherine was aware of noise and pain again. Her face was bleeding and her hand too. Her shoulder hurt but she was alive. Emergency personnel surrounded her. They were now making the attempt to remove her from the terribly crushed car. She thought of the scene she just experienced and how it had been so real to her. She had just seen James, Susie, Jimmy and Jenny and they looked so wonderful and happy. The desire to join them was overpowering but then she recalled what James had told her. As they lifted her from the car, she glanced around for the advent calendar house but it was nowhere to be seen. Perhaps it had been thrown from the car when the other car hit her. Then she recalled seeing James with an object in his hand. He was carrying the special advent calendar house back to where it came from.

It had been her special heavenly gift for twenty-four days. It had helped her travel out of a dark abyss into her own marvelous light. It had revealed what she needed to remember and what she needed to feel. In a wonderful way, it had been the catalyst to a miraculous healing of the mind and heart. Catherine suffered for years the agony of living a shallow existence, depressed and lonely in a world darkened by fear, imprisoned by her own guilt and unforgiving heart, which never could be changed by conventional medical treatment but only managed. True healing of the soul can only come when the powers of heaven intervene and the heart is willing. This can happen in anyone's heart and in the case of Catherine Daley; the miracle healing began on a cold dreary day in December. What a journey it had been, impossible to explain but true nevertheless. The joy she had once felt in her life had been tucked away deeply in her heart and was always there through every moment of despair. The calendar was the bringer of sunshine and rain to soften her heart and open it once again so it could bloom anew in the beautiful garden of life. It brought about springtime, a season of hope and rebirth during Christmastime, when the world is reminded of the birth of Him who is the source of all true hope and healing.

The Christmas Calendar had taught her the importance of not forgetting the past and not being afraid to live in the present. She remembered how to forgive and experienced being truly forgiven. She rediscovered the joy of serving others, finding and renewing friendships and embraced the great treasure of her own family relationships. It helped her remember the joy and real meaning of Christmas. She could treasure the precious memory of seeing her departed loved ones waiting anxiously for her return someday, and the comfort that brought to her heart.

The last mystery the Christmas Calendar revealed to her was her own future, which looked full of happiness. Now she thought of Doug Anderson and his family who suffered with the loss of their mother. She thought of his home with an interesting wreath on the door. Inside she could picture his living room with a beautifully decorated tree with simple decorations, a sleigh full of wrapped presents next to it, a lovely piano surrounded by the family singing Christmas carols, a simple nativity scene depicting the loving miracle and grace of God at the very first Christmas long ago and a mantle full of Christmas stockings with all the names of the Anderson family members on them including her own. It was delightful to think about. She could look forward to many wonderful Christmases to come. Now she desperately wanted to get home despite the pain she was in from the accident, spend a lovely and memorable Christmas with her family and find that phone number for Doug.

*Merry Christmas!*

CPSIA information can be obtained
at www.ICGtesting.com
Printed in the USA
FFOW01n1414071213
2583FF